THE GUNSMITH

#38

KING OF THE BORDER

Other Books
By
J.R. Roberts

For more exciting
E-Books, Audiobooks and MP3 downloads visit us at
www.speakingvolumes.us

THE GUNSMITH

#38

KING OF THE BORDER

J.R. ROBERTS

SPEAKING VOLUMES, LLC
NAPLES, FLORIDA
2014

THE GUNSMITH
#38 KING OF THE BORDER

ISBN 978-1-61232-641-2

This one is for Al Collins,
because he asked for it.

Chapter One

The Nueces Strip was a strip of land between the Rio Grande and the Nueces River, on the Texas side. John King Fisher had worked first as a cowboy in the Nueces Strip, breaking horses. During that time, however, he also cleaned some of the Mexican bandits out of the area. Later, he started his own spread, the Pendencia, and continued to clean the bandits and rustlers out of the area. He had established himself as a man of great courage, and the dominant figure in the nearby town of Eagle Pass.

Fisher did not hire ordinary cowboys on his ranch. He hired desperate men from both sides of the border, especially from Mexico, and gave them refuge and work. Everywhere he rode, his *vaqueros* followed, heavily armed and very dangerous.

Eagle Pass, Texas, became his base of operations and part of his empire. Into the situation would ride the

1

Gunsmith, unknowingly running afoul of the man everyone called "King" Fisher.

Before continuing on through Eagle Pass, Clint Adams had stopped off for the night in a town called Christianville. He put his rig, team, and Duke up at the livery, registered in a hotel, and had dinner. Later, he found a saloon, had a few drinks and a card game, and then hooked up with a willing saloon girl who said she'd meet him when she got off for the night—no charge.

When he got up the next morning, he woke her up to say good-bye.

"First you have to tell me if you remember my name," she said, putting her hands against his chest, keeping it from coming into contact with her breasts.

"Of course I remember your name."

"Then what is it?" she asked, with a grin that said she didn't believe him.

"You don't think I remember, do you?"

"No, I don't," she said, "and if you don't, you're going to leave without a farewell fuck."

He'd discovered early the night before that she liked to talk like that. At first, she appeared to think that it would shock him, but when it didn't and she continued anyway, Clint figured she did it because it excited her.

"Well in that case," he said, reaching down between her legs, "we'd better get started—Verity."

She smiled broadly and said, "You remembered!"

"How could I forget a ridiculous name like that?"

"Wha—" she started to say, but he cut her off by slipping two fingers inside of her. Her protest ended in a gasp of pleasure.

She removed her hands from his chest and ran them down his sides and hips, and then took hold of his rigid cock.

"I want it now," she said, tugging on him. "I don't like games, Clint, I like fucking!"

She tugged on him again, then slid her hands around his waist to cup his buttocks as he slid into her.

"Oh, yes!" she cried.

As he was dressing she watched, as so many women had watched before, in other hotel rooms in other towns. Clint never stayed in one place very long, but he made a point of taking care of all his pleasures wherever he stayed—gambling, women and coffee, not necessarily in that order. Invariably, when he left a town, he spent his last night with a woman, and she ended up watching him dress to leave.

"You've been through this before, haven't you?" Verity asked. She was not as young as she liked to make people believe, and she had been around long enough to know that one night in bed was not a forever proposition.

Adams looked at her, figuring her for the wrong side of thirty, although she claimed to be at least five years younger. She was blonde, blue-eyed, not beautiful but pretty, in a cheap, saloon-girl sort of way. She probably made enough money selling her favors to be able to afford to give them away when the urge struck.

"Yes, I've been through this before."

"Any of them ever cry?" she asked. "The other women, I mean?"

"On occasion." The conversation was starting to bore him. "It was nice, Verity," he said, strapping on his gun.

"Yes," she agreed, "it was. Where are you heading now?"

He knew that the next town he would come to was Eagle Pass, so he said, "Probably Eagle Pass. After that, who knows?" he added, with a shrug.

As he was heading for the door she said something that puzzled him.

"Clint, make sure you avoid King Fisher's road."

It sounded to him like the name of a street. He frowned and asked why.

She shook her head and said, "I can't tell you any more than that, Clint. Stay away from King Fisher's road. That's a warning. Remember it."

He didn't know what she was talking about, but he said, "I'll remember."

King Fisher was wearing a wide-brimmed white Mexican sombrero ornamented with gold and silver lace. His buckskin Mexican short jacket was heavily embroidered with gold. His shirt was of the finest linen, open at the throat, with a purple silk handkerchief knotted loosely about the wide collar. A brilliant crimson sash was wound around his trim waist, and his legs were hidden by a pair of wide chaps.

One of the most remarkable things about John King Fisher was that he was a young man in his early twenties. For such a young man to wield such power and demand such loyalty from the cutthroats he hired was truly remarkable.

At the moment that Clint Adams was leaving Christianville King Fisher was supervising the erection of a new wooden sign at the crossroads that led either to Eagle Pass or to his spread, the Pendencia.

"How is that, *Patron*?" one of the men asked proudly, stepping out of the way so that Fisher could see.

"That's perfect, Carlos," Fisher said. "Let's get back to the ranch."

He waited for his two men to mount up and then glanced at the sign one last time before heading back to the Pendencia.

The sign read: THIS IS KING FISHER'S ROAD—TAKE THE OTHER ONE.

Chapter Two

When Clint Adams saw the King Fisher sign, he remembered what Verity had said and turned his wagon in the direction of Eagle Pass.

Eagle Pass was not a particularly large town as border towns went, but it did appear to be a busy one. As he directed his team down the town's main street, Clint saw three men crossing the street toward the saloon, and causing all sorts of commotion as people rushed to get out of their way.

He found the livery and after making sure that the horses and rig were cared for, grabbed his saddlebags and rifle and went looking for a hotel. Border towns were usually pretty rough places, and he figured that maybe there'd be some gunsmithing business for him while he was there.

At least, he hoped so.

Nancy Ward and her brother, Douglas, ran the general store in Eagle Pass. When Douglas returned to the store from lunch, Nancy couldn't help but notice he was agitated about something.

"Doug, what's wrong?" she asked.

Douglas Ward looked at his tall, willowy sister and said, "It's just those men of King Fisher's again, walking through town like they own it. It makes me mad."

Not mad enough to *do* anything though, Nancy thought. She knew that her brother probably got out of their way as quickly as any of the others. She didn't mean to be unfair to Doug. Two men had already been killed by Fisher's men, and the law did nothing. That's because King Fisher *was* the law in Eagle Pass.

"Don't let it upset you, Doug," she said smiling.

At thirty-two, Douglas was older than his sister by five years, but it was Nancy who ran the business and made all of the decisions. All Douglas wanted to do was gamble, whenever he got his hands on enough money to do so. Nancy tried her best to keep him from losing too much of their money, but at times it had them at each other's throats.

"They upset you, don't they?" he demanded.

"Yes, but—"

"But you're a woman so no one expects *you* to do anything. Why do you expect me to risk my life by going up against them?"

"I don't, Doug."

"Yes, you do, and so does Linda." Linda was Linda McCall, the bank manager's daughter, and the woman Doug hoped to marry. "Why can't either one of you understand. Oh, the hell with it."

He turned and stalked out of the store without responding to her calls for him to come back.

Things couldn't keep on the way they were going, she decided. If Doug didn't feel so guilty about being afraid of Fisher and his men. . . . If only someone had the guts to stand up to them.

Douglas Ward headed straight for the saloon when he stormed out of his store. *His* store? he thought. Hell, it was his sister's store, they both knew that. She did all of the work, she kept them from going out of business. All he did was drink up whatever money he could get his hands on, like the five dollars he had in his pocket at that moment.

Douglas Ward intended to see just how drunk a man could get on five dollars worth of whiskey!

The Gunsmith was seated at a rear table nursing a mug of beer when he saw a young man stride purposefully into the saloon. It was clear to Clint by the look in the young man's eyes just what his purpose was. The man went right to the bar and ordered a bottle of whiskey. Clint knew by the way he grabbed at it that it might be his first, but it most definitely was not his last.

He wondered idly what it was that had driven the young man to the bottle. Women? Money? Family? Could be a hundred things. He decided to apply himself to his own beer, mind his own business, and stay out of trouble.

Those were his intentions, all right.

Chapter Three

From the way people moved out of their way Clint figured that the three men yelling and carrying on at the far side of the saloon were well known in town. They were all Mexican, wearing wide-brimmed sombreros and well-worn handguns in faded holsters. The guns were not old or ill-cared for, they were simply well used.

From where he sat the Gunsmith could see it coming, and he was determined to stay out of it.

The three Mexicans crowded over to the bar, pushing up next to the young man who was by now on his second bottle of whiskey. The Gunsmith was only on his second beer. He knew he should have gotten up and walked out of there, but he still had some of that second beer left, and he'd already paid for it.

He sat back to watch the show.

Douglas Ward knew the three Mexicans were King Fisher's men. If he'd had a gun he would have used it on the bastards—at least, that's what his whiskey-induced courage told him. It also told him that they wouldn't shoot down an unarmed man in front of a

11

room full of witnesses and that made him braver than a sober man ought to be, let alone one as drunk as he was.

"Hey, amigo," one of the Mexicans called out to the bartender. "We would like a dreenk."

But before he could answer, Doug Ward turned toward the Mexican and said, "You gonna pay for it?"

The man looked at Ward with dead eyes and said, "Are you talking to me, señor?"

"Yeah, I'm talking to you," Ward said. "You're King Fisher's men, ain't ya?"

"Si."

"That means that you'll have your drinks and then you won't pay." Ward raised his voice so that the whole room could hear him and said, "King Fisher's men never pay, they just take what they want."

The Mexican gave Ward a puzzled look and said, "We have money, señor. We will pay—"

"Nah, you won't pay," Ward said aloud. "You're all lilly-livered cowards. You're only tough when there's more than one of you."

"Señor, you are a very foolish man," he said, turning toward Ward. "You have insulted me, and you have insulted my friends."

"Yeah, so? You men are an insult to the whole town!"

The Mexican shook his head, then swung a vicious backhand that caught Ward on the right side of the face. He spun completely around and then sat down on the floor.

"Get up, señor," the Mexican said, stepping away from the bar. His two partners also stepped away, one on each side of him.

"Wha' for?''

"So my friends and I can keel you,'' the man said.

Ward looked up at them from the floor and seemed to sober up some.

"I ain't . . . ain't got a . . . a gun,'' he stammered. "You can't kill me.''

"I'm afraid, señor,'' the man said, "that we can.''

"Hold it, amigo,'' Adams called from across the room, as he stood up.

The Mexicans looked over at him.

"Señor,'' the spokesman for the Mexicans said, "this is not your fight.''

"If it was a fight,'' Clint said, "I wouldn't be interrupting, but this is starting to look like murder to me.''

"This man has insulted me and my friends,'' the Mexican said. "We have a right to take our vengeance.''

"Fairly, yes,'' Clint said, "but not this way. He's unarmed.''

"He knew he was unarmed when he attacked us with insults.''

"Still, why don't one of you meet him man to man. Give him a gun.''

The Mexican shook his head. From the corner of his eye Clint could see Ward also shaking his head.

"We will do this our way, señor,'' the man said finally. "You would do well not to interfere.''

"I know that,'' Clint said, wearily. "But I can't stand by and watch an unarmed man get killed before my eyes.''

"I am sorry, señor. You are a brave man. I apologize for having to kill you also.''

The other two men keyed on their leader. Clint guessed this and had no trouble outdrawing all three. His first bullet struck the leader in the left shoulder, spinning him around and laying him across the bar before he could reach for his gun. The other two men drew together, and Clint fired two quick shots, disarming one man and killing the other.

Doug Ward scrambled to his feet and scampered to the Gunsmith's side.

"Jeez, mister, I ain't never seen nothing that fast!"

The Mexican who had done all of the talking pushed himself off the bar and turned to face Clint unsteadily.

"You are very fast, señor."

"Fast enough."

"Si," the man said. One of his friends was on the floor dead, while the other was clutching a shattered wrist.

"You'd better get you and your friend to a doctor," Clint said. "I expect the law will be here pretty soon to take care of the body."

"The law, si," the man said, smirking. "You will have to explain yourself to the law, señor. I wish you luck."

As the man staggered out of the saloon with his partner, Clint wondered why he would have to be the one to explain himself. He had done everything he could to avoid the confrontation.

Everything, that is, except walking away.

"Señor?"

"Yes?" Clint asked, looking up from the table where he sat with Doug Ward.

"I am Sheriff Valdez, señor," the man said. A tall, slim man with a drooping mustache, he wore a star on his chest that supported this statement. "As such I must demand that you hand me your gun and accompany me to my office where I will conduct an investigation into the shooting of my brother."

"Sheriff, I can explain—" Clint started to say, but then he realized what the man had said. "Excuse me, did you say the shooting of your brother?"

"Si, señor."

Clint looked past the sheriff to the dead man on the saloon floor and asked, "Is that your brother?"

The sheriff turned and looked at the dead man.

"Oh no, that is not my brother," he said. "My brother is the man you shot in the shoulder."

Clint breathed a sigh of relief that at least he hadn't killed the lawman's brother.

"How is he?"

"The doctor has removed the bullet and says that my brother should be all right in a few weeks."

"I'm happy to hear that. I didn't want to shoot your brother, sheriff."

"We will see, señor. May I have your gun, please?"

Clint looked at the Mexican lawman and saw that he was dead serious.

"My gun?"

"Si, señor. If I find no reason to hold you for trial it will be returned to you."

"I see."

"Sheriff, this man was just helping me—" Douglas Ward spoke up.

The lawman cut him off gently. "I must ask you not to interfere, señor, or I will have to take you as well."

Ward shut up.

"Señor?" the lawman said, eyeing the Gunsmith expectantly.

"Well, since the truth is bound to come out," Clint said, and since he had no wish to be on the run from the law he took his gun from its holster and handed it to Sheriff Valdez.

"*Gracias,* señor," Valdez said, tucking the gun into his belt. "Now if you will come with me to my office?"

"Of course, Sheriff."

Clint rose and preceded the lawman from the saloon, wishing that for once he'd been able to mind his own damn business.

Chapter Four

When they reached the sheriff's office Clint found that it was a one-room, adobe structure with no jail cell.

"This is where we will conduct our investigation," Sheriff Valdez announced. "Please sit."

"What form will this investigation take?"

"You speak as if you were once—"

"I was a lawman for a long time," Clint explained, interrupting Valdez. "But that was sometime ago."

"I see."

"Do you have a judge in town?"

"Unfortunately, no."

"A circuit judge?"

"We are not on a route."

"Then what kind of investigation will you conduct?"

"I will ask you questions, and you will answer. From your answers I will decide your guilt."

"You will pass judgment?"

"I will decide if you should be held for trial."

17

"And if you decide that I should, what then?"

The Mexican lawman scratched his head and said, "I do not know exactly. I suppose I will have to find someplace to hold you until we can get a judge to come to town."

"How long would that be?"

The man shrugged and said, "I do not know."

Clint frowned. "Since it was your brother I shot, how fair can I expect you to be?"

Valdez just shrugged.

"Ask your questions then."

The lawman proceeded to ask Clint why he had shot his brother. The Gunsmith explained the circumstances leading up to the incident.

"You outdrew three men?"

"That's right."

Valdez looked surprised. "It seems to me you interfered in business that was not your own. You injured my brother and another man, and killed a third."

"I can't argue that."

"I can only find that you must be held for trial."

"Isn't there something—some understanding that we can come to?"

"What do you suggest?"

"Since you don't have a jail to keep me in, why don't I just give you my word that I won't leave town until a judge arrives to preside over my trial."

"Your word?"

"Yes, as an ex-lawman."

The sheriff rubbed his jaw and said, "You could run when I release you."

"It would be up to you to accept my word."

Valdez frowned in annoyance. Obviously he had never been presented with such decisions before.

"I'd also have to have my gun."

"I could not return it to you."

"I'm sure your brother and his friends have friends who will not like what happened. I'd have to be able to protect myself."

Suddenly the Gunsmith knew that he had pushed too hard in asking that his gun be returned.

"I could not take the chance that you might kill someone else. I will just have to find a place to hold you."

"Some place with a soft mattress, I hope." Clint Adams said.

Sheriff Valdez took out an old set of shackles and fastened Clint's wrist to the chair he was seated in. Then he left to make the arrangements for his prisoner. Clint knew he could have shattered that chair to pieces and escaped, but he decided to play the hand out the way it had been dealt.

Valdez returned shortly with a puzzled look on his face and told the Gunsmith, "You are a very lucky man."

"How's that?"

"My brother does not wish to press charges against you for shooting him."

"That's interesting," Clint said. "Did your brother give you a reason?"

"He said that you acted honorably and coura-geously, and outdrew him and his two men fairly."

"You're letting me go, then?"

"Si."

Valdez released Clint from his shackles and then returned his gun to him.

"I would not look very pleased about this," the lawman said, and it sounded like a warning.

"Why not?" Clint asked, putting on his gunbelt.

"My brother and his *compadres* are King Fisher's men," Valdez said. "Señor Fisher will have much to say about you shooting three of his men."

"Is that a fact?"

"Also, the rest of my brother's compadres will feel that it is their duty to avenge him and the others."

"I see," Clint said. "Then what you're telling me is that I am jumping from the frying pan into the fire."

"That is very good, señor," the lawman said, raising his eyebrows. "If I were you, Señor Adams, I would be very careful that I did not get burned."

Chapter Five

On his way out of the sheriff's office Clint bumped into a young woman who appeared to be in something of a hurry.

"Excuse me," he said, holding her by the shoulders to steady her. She was a pretty thing with long brown hair, and there was something familiar about her.

"I'm sorry," she said, looking past him, "I was in a hurry to catch—" She stopped short then and moved her gaze to his face. "Are you the man who helped my brother?"

"Your brother?"

"My name is Nancy Ward. My brother is Douglas."

"Oh, the young man who tried to take on three of King Fisher's vaqueros with his mouth."

Her jaw firmed up. She nodded shortly and said, "That's my brother. Who are you?"

"I'm Clint Adams," he said, admiring her clear brown eyes.

21

"Adams, yes, that's what he said your name was. I hurried over to see if I could help."

"Well, that was very nice of you, Miss Ward, but as you can see I'm not in immediate need of assistance."

"You mean the sheriff let you free?"

"He did."

"But I understood one of the men you shot was his brother," she said, looking puzzled.

"He was."

"I don't understand. Then why did he let you go?"

"Apparently his brother doesn't want to press charges."

Her eyes narrowed and she said, "That's probably King Fisher's doing."

"Why do you say that?"

"King Fisher—"

"Excuse me, but could I walk you somewhere? I'd rather not talk in front of the sheriff's office. No telling when he might change his mind."

"Of course," she said. "You could walk me to my store, if you'd be so kind."

"I'd be happy to."

As they walked Clint said, "Tell me about King Fisher."

"You must come from another territory if you don't know about King Fisher," she said with feeling. "He's a young man with a lot of power, and I think it has corrupted him."

"Why did you say that it was his doing that I'm free right now?"

"He probably ordered his man, the sheriff's brother, not to press charges because Fisher wants you free, where he could get at you."

"He or his men?"

"Probably his men, but as I understand it, if he wanted to do his dirty work himself, he could." They stopped in front of the general store.

"This is our store. My brother is in the back lying down. He's still pretty shaken up."

"I would imagine."

She turned to look at Clint speculatively and asked, "Did you really outdraw three men?"

"They weren't very fast," he said, playing it down.

"Yes, but still, to outdraw three men—"

"You've got to be pretty lucky, which I was," he said, quickly. "One good thing came out of this, however."

"Really? What?"

"The incident sobered your brother up pretty quickly."

"He'll find another excuse to drink," she said, and then her hand flew to her mouth as if she hadn't meant to say it. "I'm sorry. I must go inside and open the store. We can't stay closed for very long, or we'll lose too much money."

"I appreciate your closing up your store to rush to my aid."

"It was the least that I could do." She unlocked the door and then turned back to face him. "Will you be leaving town now?"

"I hadn't intended to."

"You'll be in danger if you stay."

"Maybe."

"Well, good luck, whatever you decide."

They stood facing each other awkwardly for a few moments and then she said, "I really must go inside."

"Perhaps we'll see each other again."

"That . . . would be nice," she said and went inside.

Inside the store Nancy Ward leaned against the counter and wondered if a man had finally come to town who would be able to stand against King Fisher.

Chapter Six

The Gunsmith was having breakfast the next morning in the small dining room of the hotel where he was staying when suddenly the room, which had been filled with murmured conversations from other tables, fell totally silent.

Standing at the front entrance to the dining room was a somewhat flamboyantly dressed young man, flanked by vaqueros in trail clothes. They looked much like the men Clint had shot in the saloon.

The mustachioed young man started forward toward Clint's table, and the vaqueros followed. Other diners leaned away from their path.

The man was very obviously King Fisher, and as he reached Clint's table the Gunsmith poured an extra cup of coffee.

''I've been expecting you,'' he said to King Fisher. ''Have a cup of coffee.''

The offer had the desired effect on the powerful, young rancher. It threw him off balance, but he impressed the Gunsmith by regaining his composure almost immediately.

"Gracias," he said, although he was plainly not Mexican, but American.

"Could you send these two to another table—or another town?" Clint asked, eyeing Fisher's vaqueros.

Fisher instructed his men to wait outside.

"You're the Gunsmith," Fisher said then.

"My name is Clint Adams."

"You're also the Gunsmith," Fisher said. "You can't be one without being the other."

"That is right."

Fisher sipped his coffee, taking it black the way Clint did.

"As I understand it, you outdrew three of my men yesterday, killing one and disabling the other two."

"That's the way it happened, all right."

"You've cost me some men then, and some time."

"I gave your men a fair chance at walking away," Clint offered.

"I'm sure that if they had realized who you were, they would have," Fisher said. "As it stands, you owe me."

"And you're here to collect?"

"That's right."

"I'm sorry," Clint said, "but I've got nothing to give you in return for your men."

"Yes, you have."

Clint put down his knife and fork, picked up his cup of coffee, and said, "I think you'll have to explain that."

"Gladly. My men expect me to back them, no matter what the situation. They expect me to kill you."

"Or have me killed," Clint said, just to let the man know that he'd heard stories about him.

Fisher ignored the remark.

"I would rather not kill you," he said. "I would prefer that you come and work for me."

"Replace the three men I cost you?"

"That's right."

"You think your men will go for that?"

"They'll do what I tell them."

"I'd be walking right into the lion's den, wouldn't I?" Clint asked. "One of those men would have to try and kill me."

"That would be your problem," Fisher said, finishing his coffee and preparing to stand.

"How long would this be for?"

Fisher stood up and said, "For as long as I say, naturally."

"I'm afraid the answer is no, Fisher," Clint said. "I won't work for you."

"Think it over," Fisher advised.

"I don't have to."

"I think you might have misunderstood me," Fisher said. "I'd prefer not to kill you, but I really wouldn't mind much one way or the other."

"I still won't work for you."

Now Fisher shrugged and said, "In that case I'd leave town if I were you."

Clint hated when people told him to leave town. He didn't want his reputation as the Gunsmith, but it was something that he had to live with, and he couldn't very well leave town every time someone told him to. That would set him up as a target for every young gun-tough in the West.

"I'll keep it under advisement," he said. He picked up his knife and fork and pointedly ignored Fisher's departure.

Outside, Fisher's two vaqueros were waiting patiently for Fisher to reappear.

"Patron?" Carlos asked.

"Let us go see how your compadres are," Fisher said.

"Valdez and Dominguez?" the other man said.

Fisher glared at him, and the man looked away.

"Who else, *stupido*," Carlos snapped. "Patron, what about the gringo?"

"I guess we'll have to talk about that, Carlos," Fisher said to his foreman.

Chapter Seven

Clint Adams had originally intended to leave Eagle Pass fairly soon, but now knew that he was going to have to chance spending at least a few days there. He hoped that at the end of that time he'd still be alive.

He spent the bulk of that day trying to drum up some gunsmithing business, attempting to make the stay in Eagle Pass worthwhile. The only other thing he could think of that might have made the stay worth it was getting to know Nancy Ward a little better. Well, make that a lot better.

He was inside his rig working on a Navy Colt with a worn firing pin when someone knocked. He moved to the door, opened it, and found himself looking into the fair-skinned face of a lovely, young blonde girl.

"Hi," she said, brightly. She couldn't have been more than nineteen. She had wide, blue eyes and long hair the color of wheat. Her body was full-breasted and slim-hipped. Clint had found something else that would make his stay in Eagle Pass more bearable.

"Hello," he said, stepping down to the ground. The

girl was tall, standing as high as Clint's eyes. "Can I help you?"

"You certainly can," she said, looking him up and down candidly.

When she did not elaborate he asked, "How?"

"I have a gun . . . that needs repairing."

"May I see it?"

"Of course."

From a drawstring purse she produced a small, single-shot .32 caliber derringer.

"What's the problem with it?"

"I don't know, really," she said. "All I know is that it won't fire."

"Is it yours?"

"No, why?"

"I was just wondering if you were in the habit of carrying it in your purse."

"Would that affect the way it works?"

"No," Clint said. "I was just curious. Who does the gun belong to?"

"My father," she said. "He's the manager of the bank here in Eagle Pass."

"I see."

"He keeps the gun in his desk, but lately he's been saying how he should get it repaired, and I thought that with you in town it was an ideal opportunity."

"Makes sense."

They stared at each other for a few moments, and then she asked, "Can you fix it?"

"Probably. I'll need some time to look at it. Why don't you come back later this afternoon. Perhaps I'll know by then."

"All right, I will."

They stared for another few seconds, and then she started to back away, saying, "I guess I'll get going. I have work to do."

"Do you work in the bank, too?"

"Oh, yes. I'm a teller."

"What's your name?"

"Linda," she said, "Linda McCall."

"All right, Miss McCall. I'll see you later this evening."

"Right," she said, still backing towards the door. "Thank you."

"Thank *you*."

She bumped into one of the livery stable doors, waved at him and then left.

Clint had the distinct feeling that he had been looked over. He wondered what the verdict had been.

On his way to the livery stable to renew acquaintances with the man who had saved his life, Douglas Ward saw Linda McCall slip out of the barn and trot off toward the bank. She was so beautiful, and she reminded him of a young filly cantering about in a field.

It was only after she turned the corner that he wondered what she'd been doing in the livery stable with Clint Adams. He changed his mind about seeing Adams and headed back to the store.

King Fisher was angry, and his foreman, Carlos DeJesus, was fearful.

"Patron, it is very difficult when the man we are dealing with is the Gunsmith."

Fisher glared at Carlos and then relented, admitting to himself that it was not the foreman's fault he couldn't find any vaqueros to go up against Adams, not after the Gunsmith had already outdrawn three of his best men.

"Very well, Carlos," Fisher said. "We will have to try something else."

"Shall I get out my rifle?"

Fisher knew that if he told Carlos to get his rifle, the Gunsmith would be dead sometime over the next few days of a bullet in the back.

"No," he said, "not that way. He has embarrassed me, and he must be taught a lesson that everyone will say is fair."

"But none of our men will face him fairly."

"You would, Carlos," Fisher said, staring at his foreman, "if I asked you to. Wouldn't you?"

"It would be instant death," Carlos said warily, and then added, "but for you, Patron, I would. Si."

Fisher smiled and said, "You are loyal, Carlos."

"Si, Patron."

"Don't worry, I won't ask this of you."

Carlos silently thanked the Lord.

"We will find someone," Fisher said, "someone good, and fast, someone with a reputation just as big as the Gunsmith's."

"But where will we find such a man?" Carlos asked.

"That, Carlos," Fisher said, regarding his foreman with a shrug, "is a good question."

It took Douglas Ward a couple of hours to work up

the nerve, but finally he entered the bank and approached the teller's window, behind which stood Linda McCall.

"Hello, Linda."

The pretty, blue-eyed girl looked up and Ward saw her smile. Of course, that was all he wanted to see. What he didn't see was the tolerant look that preceded the smile. Linda McCall tolerated Douglas Ward because she knew he was in love with her, and she knew that he and his sister owned a business in town. She didn't love him, but she didn't want to close any doors prematurely, so she was nice to him.

"Hi, Douglas."

"Are you busy?"

It was very easy for anyone to see that the bank was not crowded at that time of day, but she sighed and said, "Not very."

"I was just wondering if you would like to, uh, have dinner with me tonight, after work?"

Immediately she thought of Clint Adams and said, "Oh, I'm afraid I can't tonight. I'll be busy."

She hoped.

When she had gone to see Clint Adams she had done so not to get her father's gun fixed—although it did need fixing—but because she had heard that "the Gunsmith" was in town, and she wanted to meet him. It wasn't everyday that a girl got to see a legend, and once she had seen him she hoped that he would ask her to have dinner with him. Perhaps he would, when she went back to pick up the gun, but she had to be free to say yes.

"Not tonight?"

"I'm sorry, Douglas."

"No, that's all right," Ward said. "We can do it another time."

"You're sweet," she said, because she knew that he liked it when she told him that.

"I'll let you get back to work now."

"Thank you, Douglas."

As he left the bank, Linda McCall immediately forgot him and started thinking about Clint Adams again.

The problem with the banker's derringer was the problem with many guns Clint Adams had repaired in the past: neglect. By the time Linda McCall appeared to reclaim it, he had cleaned and oiled it, and it was working perfectly.

He explained this to her prior to returning it, and then added, "Your father is going to have to take better care of this gun in the future. That means taking it out of the desk drawer once in a while and cleaning it."

"I'll make sure I tell him," she said, taking the gun and putting it back in her drawstring purse.

"Miss McCall."

"Yes."

"I was wondering if you could tell a stranger if there was a decent place to eat in town."

Linda McCall decided that this was her opening, and she was going to take it.

"There is a place," she said, "but it would be better if I showed you."

"Well," the Gunsmith said, "that was my next question."

She smiled and said, "Well then, consider it asked and answered."

"Would you mind if I cleaned up first?"

"Of course not," she said. "I've only just finished work myself. Why don't we meet in your hotel lobby in, say, an hour?"

"That's fine," he said. "I'll see you then."

"Good," she said, smiling widely.

As before she backed away until she reached the door, and then scampered through it.

As Linda McCall walked toward the house she shared with her father, she did not see a rather drunken Douglas Ward following her. A few drinks under his belt had enabled him to work up the courage to follow her from the bank after work. He suspected that she'd be meeting with Clint Adams that night, and now he knew for sure. She puzzled him by leaving alone and heading home. He intended to follow her and see what she did next. If she was going home to change to meet Adams again, then he was going to need a few more drinks to teach the Gunsmith that saving a man's life did not give him the right to steal a man's girl.

Chapter Eight

When Clint met Linda in the small lobby of his hotel he was impressed. For a girl so young she had a commanding presence, especially when she was dressed up. The dress she was wearing was fairly modest, in good taste, yet it showed her figure off to its best advantage.

"You look lovely," he'd said honestly.

"Thank you."

In fact, she looked so lovely that Clint wished he'd had some finer clothes to wear himself. The clothes he was wearing were clean, but they were still trail clothes.

"You look very handsome."

"Now that we've got that out of the way," he'd said, "why don't we go and eat."

"And get that out of the way, too?" she'd asked with raised eyebrows, her meaning more than clear.

They returned to his hotel after dinner and, with unspoken agreement, walked up to his room.

"I can't wait any longer," she'd said, unfastening

her dress and letting it drop to the floor. "I want you inside of me."

She discarded her undergarments and stood before him gloriously naked. Her breasts were round and firm, with pink nipples that had already become hard with passion. Clint expected her passion to be totally unbridled once they got into bed.

She watched him undress and then opened her arms to him as he stepped towards her. Their mouths had fused together, tongues eagerly entwining, and his hands sought out her firm breasts, palmed them, squeezed them, enjoying the hard, little nubs of her nipples as they pressed against his palms.

He guided her to the edge of the mattress and she fell onto the bed with him on top of her. Quickly, she swiveled around so that she was on top. She flattened her hands against his chest and started grinding herself down against him, taking him as deeply inside of her as she could. Her eyes were closed, her head thrown back.

Outside, Douglas Ward waited across the street in a darkened doorway, taking an occasional swig from the half-empty whiskey bottle he held cradled in his arms.

She had turned the tables on him so expertly that Clint guessed she was used to getting her way in bed. She needed a lesson from a strong man, and the Gunsmith was only too happy to oblige her.

Her eyes were still closed when he took her by the waist and lifted her off of him and onto her back.

"Wha—" she gasped, her eyes opened in surprise.

"You've had your way long enough, Linda," he said, moving astride her. "Now it's my turn."

"But—" she said, frowning slightly.

"Relax," he told her, and in one swift movement his head was nestled between her legs, his tongue expertly flicking at her moist womanhood.

"Oh, Clint . . ." she gasped, grabbing his head as his tongue lapped at her hot juices. She wrapped her fingers in his hair as his tongue suddenly slid inside of her, causing her hips to jump off the bed of their own accord.

"Jesus," she moaned, aware that for the first time in her young life she was losing control of herself.

Suddenly his lips closed on her rigid little love bud, and she became dizzy as her body was wracked by huge spasms of pure pleasure.

"God . . . help . . ." she muttered as she lost control of her emotions, her body and her mind.

Douglas Ward was becoming a very impatient young man, but as he stepped out of his doorway he drunkenly lost his footing and fell onto his behind. Now seated on the doorstep, he decided that another drink from his bottle was in order before he went across the street to find out what was going on.

Linda McCall had barely recovered from the dizzying effects of Clint Adams' oral stimulations when his thick, pulsing penis plunged deep inside of her, forcing a cry of delight from her. He reached beneath her to cup her slim buttocks and pull her tightly against him. In addition to everything else, Linda's tender, sensitive nipples were being scraped by Clint's chest hairs.

"Oh Clint . . . God . . . I've never felt anything like this—"

He silenced her by covering her mouth with his, at the same time stoking the fire in her loins with long, slow thrusts.

Suddenly she was bucking beneath him, moaning into his mouth, raking his back with her nails, and wrapping her long, powerful thighs around his waist. When she felt the burning needles of his semen flooding into her, she once again became dizzily unaware of her surroundings.

Linda McCall was still unsteady on her legs as Clint Adams walked her back to her house a few hours later.

"What will your father think about you coming home this late?" he asked.

"Don't worry about that," she said, leaning against him. "Worry about how he's going to react when I don't show up for work in the morning."

"Why not?"

"I don't know if I'll be able to. Clint Adams, I have never had a man do to me what you did to me tonight."

"Complaining?"

She grinned tiredly and said, "Not complaining, Mr. Adams, but I think I deserve a rematch."

"Anytime, Linda."

She kissed him swiftly and said, "Next time I'll be ready for you," and went inside.

Walking back to his hotel Clint suddenly became

aware of movement in a doorway across the street. Peering into the darkness he moved closer and finally saw Douglas Ward sprawled in the doorway.

"Ward?" he said.

"Yuh," the man replied, drunkenly. One bleary eye opened, and the man looked up at Clint Adams. "You!" he snapped.

"I don't know if you know who I am or not," Clint said, "but I think I'd better get you home. Your sister is probably worried about you."

"Sister," the man mumbled, "worried . . ."

"Come on, Ward," Clint said, reaching down to help the man to his feet. He pulled on Ward's arm, but as the drunken man came to his feet he swung his right fist at the Gunsmith's jaw.

"Whoa!" Clint called, ducking under the slow, clumsily thrown blow. Ward fell over Clint's shoulder, and the Gunsmith carried him home.

Hefting the slim young man on his shoulder, adjusting to the man's weight, Clint carried him all the way to the general store, where he used his foot to bang on the door. He only hoped that Nancy Ward would be able to hear him from the back. When a light glowed inside, he knew that she had.

"What—" the young woman asked as she opened the door and peered out, bleary-eyed. She had obviously been asleep, but when she saw Clint Adams bearing her brother like a sack of flour her eyes opened wide, and she came fully awake.

"What happened?"

"He's had a little too much to drink, I think," Clint said.

"Where was he?"

"Sitting in a doorway across from my hotel."

"What was he doing there?"

"I don't rightly know, Miss Ward, but perhaps we could talk about it after I put him down? He looks light enough, but try holding him for more than five minutes."

"Oh, I'm sorry," she said, backing up. "Please, bring him in the back."

As Clint entered Nancy pulled her housedress together at the neck, but not before he caught a glimpse of a swell of creamy, white breast.

"The back?"

"Straight back and to the right," she directed him. "That's his room."

Clint followed her direction, carried Douglas Ward into the back and dropped him on his unmade bed.

"I didn't have a chance to make his bed today," she said, coming in behind him.

"No need to explain to me," Clint said, pausing to catch his breath.

"Is he all right?" she asked, gazing down at her brother with concern wrinkling her brow.

"He's fine, ma'am. He just drank too damn much—if you'll excuse my language."

"Don't excuse yourself," she said. "I've heard much worse. I'm sorry you had to go through this."

"It was no problem, really," he said. "I just didn't think he should be sleeping out in the street. Maybe in the morning you'll be able to find out the reason for this."

"Probably the same thing that always drives him to the bottle," she said sadly.

"What's that?"

She paused, as if she wasn't sure she should answer, and then said, "Oh, his own weaknesses, and probably Linda McCall."

"Linda McCall?" Clint asked, attempting to do so casually.

"Yes, she's the bank manager's daughter, and I'm afraid my brother has foolishly fallen in love with her."

"Why foolishly?"

"Oh, she's young and beautiful, and I don't think she intends to settle for one man for quite a while." It was clear by her tone and the look on her face that Nancy Ward did not approve of Linda McCall. "She's a little wild, but Doug won't see that. He only sees in her what he wants to see."

"I guess that's as good a definition of a man in love as there will ever be."

She looked at him with interest and then said, "I suppose it is."

There was an awkward silence between them and then he said, "Well, I'll let you get to bed, Miss Ward."

"Please, call me Nancy. It's a small enough thing to ask after what you've done for my brother—and for me—since you came to town."

"All right, Nancy. Maybe before I leave we can find another way for you to repay me," he said, his intention innocent enough.

"Like how?" she asked, and he immediately became aware of the suspicion on her face. He would have to be very careful with this one. She'd been spooked before.

"Perhaps a dinner together."

"Oh," she said, and then added, "I think that would be nice."

"We'll see about it later, then. Good night, Nancy."

"Good night . . . Clint."

She followed him to the front and locked the door behind him.

Adams went back to his hotel wondering just how long Ward had been sitting in that doorway.

Chapter Nine

Texas Ranger Captain Lee McNelly paced the confines of his office, pausing every so often to cough violently into a white linen handkerchief. He had just experienced another spasm when there was a knock on his door.

"Yes?"

His aide, Ranger Cliff Fricke, entered carrying a steaming cup of tea on a tray.

"Your tea, Cap'n."

"I didn't ask for any tea, damn it!" McNelly snapped testily.

"I know you didn't, sir," Fricke said, turning to face his superior. Fricke was barely old enough to shave, yet McNelly had to admit that he made a good aide, except for his annoying habit of "mothering" him. "But your cough has not been getting any better, so I added some honey to this one."

"Fine, fine. Just leave it," McNelly said. He hadn't the heart to tell his young aide that neither tea nor honey was a cure for tuberculosis.

"Yes, sir," Fricke said, assuming his kicked-dog look.

"And Fricke."

"Yessir?"

"Thank you."

Fricke smiled and said, "You're welcome, sir."

After Fricke left the room Captain McNelly ambled over to his desk and began to sip systematically at the tea, solely to appease his young aide. While sipping he was thinking about the largest of the many thorns in his side, John King Fisher.

Fisher's hold on the border town of Eagle Pass and the area surrounding the town and his ranch, the Pendencia, was ironclad, and the worse thing about the whole situation was that it was legal. McNelly could not find anything to move on, even though he knew Fisher's hold over the Nueces Strip was built on corruption and fear.

Still, his own personal knowledge of this was not enough. He needed some evidence to act on, and right now only one man was in a position to get it for him.

Clint Adams.

The Texas Rangers had had dealings with the Gunsmith in the past, most recently regarding the border bandit known as Gila,* but their relationship had been something less than amiable. Ever since McNelly had learned of Adams' presence in Eagle Pass, he had felt sure that the Gunsmith was his only hope of putting King Fisher where he belonged—behind bars.

McNelly was about to drink the last of his tea when

_____

*The Gunsmith #34: Night of the Gila

another coughing fit seized him, causing the cup to fall from his hand. It shattered against the floor as the captain groped for his handkerchief.

This plan had to pay off, because there was no telling if he'd ever have another.

Carlos DeJesus did not have good news for King Fisher, and he did not relish having to tell him so.

"Come in, Carlos," Fisher said, as the foreman appeared at the door of his office. "What news do you have for me?"

"I have sent telegrams," Carlos said timidly, "but have not yet found a man such as the one we need."

King Fisher took the news much better than Carlos DeJesus had thought.

"Carlos, I may just have to do this thing myself."

"Before I would let you do such a thing, I would give my own life, Patron."

"There's that loyalty again, Carlos," Fisher said with something akin to affection. "Keep looking, my friend. Keep looking."

"Si, Patron."

As Carlos DeJesus turned to leave Fisher called out his name again.

"Patron?"

"What have we heard from our friend Captain McNelly?"

Carlos made a face that mirrored his distaste for McNelly and said, "The Rangers have been quiet."

"Yes, well, that's when they're the most dangerous, isn't it?"

"Si, Patron."

"That's all, Carlos."

After Fricke had cleaned up the shattered pieces of the cup and removed them, Captain McNelly told him to come back into the office.

"I need a man to go into Eagle Pass in plain clothes, Fricke," McNelly said.

"I'm ready, sir," Fricke said eagerly.

McNelly laughed and said, "I wasn't thinking of sending you, Fricke."

"Oh," Fricke said, obviously disappointed.

"Who do we have available?"

"Well, Richmond and Roe are in Arizona. . . ." Fricke replied and went on to explain that there weren't very many men who were available for this assignment.

McNelly stared at Fricke and wondered if he dared send the lad into Eagle Pass.

Chapter Ten

Clint Adams was once again having breakfast in the hotel dining room when he saw a young man enter and anxiously look about the room. When his eyes fell on the Gunsmith his face brightened, and he started across the room. As he reached Clint's table the Gunsmith noticed that he was a few years older than he appeared to be.

"Are you Clint Adams?"

"That's right."

"Can I sit down?"

"That depends."

"On what?"

"On what you're selling."

The lad grinned and said, "Oh, I ain't selling nothing, Mr. Adams."

"Then why do you want to sit down?"

"I got to talk to you." The lad looked around nervously and said, "It would be easier if I were allowed to sit, sir."

The way the young man said "sir" sent a chill up the

Gunsmith's spine. Only a soldier said that word in quite that way—a soldier or a Texas Ranger.

"Sit," Clint said, gesturing with the knife he was using to cut his steak.

"Thank you, sir."

"And stop calling me 'sir.' "

"Yessi—uh, yes."

He sat down and stared at Clint's plate.

"Have you eaten?"

"No s—no."

Clint motioned for the waiter to come over and instructed him to bring a second plate.

"While we're waiting for your breakfast to arrive, why don't you tell me your name?"

"Fricke, sir," the lad said, pronouncing it Frick-*E*, "Cliff Fricke."

"Private Fricke," Clint asked, "or Ranger Fricke?"

Fricke frowned and said, "It's Ranger Fricke, sir, but how did you know?"

"It's that word," Clint said.

"What word?" Fricke asked, frowning again.

" 'Sir,' " Clint said. "It's the way you say it. You have to be either a soldier or a Ranger."

"Really? That's very smart of you."

"Clint."

"Sir?"

The Gunsmith gave the lad an exasperated look and said, "Not sir, Clint."

"Oh, I see. All right . . . Clint."

At that point the waiter arrived with Ranger Fricke's breakfast, and the young man proceeded to devour it with gusto.

"Can you talk and eat at the same time?"

"Sure."

"Why don't you tell me why you're here then?"

Fricke nodded, chewed vigorously, swallowed, and said, "All right. I've been sent here in secret to speak to you on behalf of the Texas Rangers."

"Who sent you?"

"Captain McNelly."

"Don't know him."

"Well, he knows of you." Suddenly a worried look came over the young Ranger's face, and he leaned forward and asked, "You are the Gunsmith aren't you?"

"I've been called that."

"Oh," Fricke said, relief plain on his face. "Well, the captain would like to request your help in acquiring evidence against one John Fisher, otherwise known as King Fisher."

"Is that a fact? What kind of evidence?"

That stopped Fricke in mid-chew as he screwed up his face and then admitted, "He didn't tell me that—exactly."

"Just what is Captain McNelly after King Fisher for?"

Fricke shrugged and said, "Anything, I reckon. Anything he can get on him. He just feels—knows, actually—that King Fisher isn't a true and honest man."

Clint stared at the Ranger and asked, "Were those Captain McNelly's exact words?"

"Uh, no. They're my own words," the lad said humbly. "But that's the way the captain feels."

"Why don't you tell me exactly what this Captain

McNelly wants of me, Cliff.''

"Well sir—well, he'd just like you to take notice of King Fisher's activities and let him know as soon as you think something, uh, illegal is going on.''

"And how am I supposed to let him know? Send a telegram to the Texas Rangers from King Fisher's town?''

"No, si—Clint. Why, that'd be downright dumb, wouldn't it?''

"Downright.''

"No, as soon as you spot something you're to tell me, and I'll take the information to Cap'n McNelly.''

"You're staying in Eagle Pass?''

"That's right.''

"Then why don't *you* observe?''

"I'm, uh, sort of inexperienced in field work,'' Fricke admitted, looking embarrassed.

"Well, what better way for you to *get* some experience then sending you into the lion's den, right?'' Clint asked, wondering what in hell had ever possessed a captain of the Texas Rangers to send a boy like this into Eagle Pass.

"The lion's den?'' Fricke asked, looking worried. "Is there a lion around here, Clint?''

"Eat your breakfast, Fricke,'' Clint said. "It's getting cold.''

The first thing Clint had to do was put Fricke someplace where he wouldn't get hurt. Out of town seemed to make the most sense.

Over coffee he told the young Ranger, "Look, go back to your Captain McNelly and tell him I've got my own business with King Fisher, and when that's taken care of, I'm leaving Eagle Pass. I don't have time to play games for the Texas Rangers. Understand?''

"But the captain thinks you're his only chance of finally catching Fisher," Fricke argued, looking worried. "You gotta help him."

"No, I don't," Clint said. "I was a lawman a long time ago, but that's over now, and I don't intend to go back to it."

"Nobody's asking you to sign up—"

"Not formally, maybe, but that's what it amounts to. No, I'm sorry, Cliff, but you tell your captain that he'd better get himself another boy—and you better get your butt out of town. You don't belong here."

"I'm a Ranger," Fricke said, drawing himself up in his chair.

"That's right," Clint said. "But you are in need of a little more seasoning."

Fricke stood up stiffly and said, "Thank you for your time, Mr. Adams."

"Get out of town, Cliff," the Gunsmith said, "get out of Eagle Pass before you get hurt."

Chapter Eleven

Clint was back in his rig working. He was thinking about Linda McCall and Douglas Ward.

As if he didn't have enough problems, he now had to
deal with the goddamn Texas Rangers' wanting to
recruit him to come up with evidence—any kind of
evidence—against King Fisher.

The ideal thing would be for him to leave town now
and forget all about all of them, but his goddamn
reputation wouldn't allow that. As it was, he was a
target for would-be gunmen, but if it ever got out that
he had been forced out of Eagle Pass . . .

No, he was going to have to wait King Fisher out.
The reprisal would come, and when it was over—
hopefully without anyone else dying—then he'd
leave town. Meanwhile, all of these people—Linda,
Nancy, Douglas, Fisher, Fricke, and even Captain

McNelly—were part of his life, and he was going to have to deal with them, one by one.

"Adams had a visitor at breakfast," Carlos De-Jesus informed his boss.

"Who?"

"We don't know for sure," Carlos said. "A young gringo who just rode into town and went directly to the Gunsmith's hotel."

"Then he came into town specifically to talk to Clint Adams."

"That is the way it seems."

"Where is this young gringo now?"

"He took a room in the other hotel."

"All right. I want a man watching him and a man watching Adams at all times."

"Si, Patron."

"And I want constant reports on their move-ments—especially Adams. If it looks like he's going to leave town, I'll have to kill him myself."

"That could possibly leave you open to charges from the Texas Rangers, Patron."

"True."

"Captain McNelly would be very grateful for that."

"I would have to take that chance, Carlos. No man, not even the Gunsmith, must be able to come into my town, shoot three of my men, and ride away without reprisal."

"I understand."

"Go now. Make sure both men are watched constantly—and I don't care if they know it."

"As you wish."

When Carlos left John King Fisher strapped on his
ivory-handled, silver-plated revolvers and wondered if
he would be able to outdraw the legendary Gunsmith.

Chapter Twelve

"I want you to tell me what happened last night?"
Nancy Ward asked her brother.

"Never mind," he said sullenly. "I'd like another
cup of coffee."

"Get it yourself, then," she said, standing up and
beginning to clear the table. "I've got a store to run."

"That's right," Douglas Ward said. "You run the
store, but that doesn't mean you get to run my *life*."

"I'm not trying to run your life, Doug," she said.
"I'd simply like you to start living it in a worthwhile
manner."

"I am."

"You call mooning around about Linda McCall
worthwhile?" she demanded. "She doesn't love you,
Doug. She doesn't even care about you."

"That's not true!" he shouted, leaping to his feet.

"Douglas, why were you lying drunk in a doorway
last night? Does it have something to do with Linda
McCall?"

"I'm going out."

"Or Clint Adams?"

He glared at her, and she thought that perhaps she had hit on it.

"Why him?" Douglas asked.

"He found you last night and carried you home."

"Found me?"

"In a doorway across from his hotel. He was nice enough to carry you home."

"Sure, nice enough," Douglas snapped. "Maybe now he'll feel justified in going after my sister."

As Douglas stormed out she stared after him wondering what he meant by that.

"Why do you want to buy a gun from me, Douglas?" Mendez asked. Rafael Mendez ran the gunshop in Eagle Pass. "You sell them at the store, don't you?"

"I don't want one from my—my sister's store," Douglas Ward said. "I want to buy one from you."

Mendez narrowed his eyes and asked, "You got money?"

"Ah, I'll need a little credit, Mr. Mendez."

The old Mexican shook his head sadly and said, "I do not do business that way, Douglas. You know that."

"Mr. Mendez—"

"I am sorry, Douglas."

As Douglas Ward started to leave Mendez called out, "What do you need a gun for, anyway?"

When Nancy Ward found out from Mendez that her brother had been trying to buy a gun, she locked away all of the guns in her own store, and then went to find Clint Adams.

"Clint?"

The door to his rig was open and when he looked back he saw Nancy Ward's face peering in.

"I'll come out," he said, putting down the gun he was working on.

"I'm sorry to bother you," she said as he stepped out of his rig.

"No bother."

"It's Douglas."

"What happened now?"

"I don't know, that's the problem," she said. "I found out that he's been trying to buy a gun."

"Well, he hasn't tried to buy one off of me. Don't you sell them in your store?"

"Yes, but I think he wanted to get one without my knowing it. I've locked up the guns in the store, but I'm worried he still might get a hold of one."

"Why does he want a gun?"

"I don't know. I thought it might have something to do with either you or Linda McCall."

"Oh," he said.

She peered at him curiously, and he hoped that he didn't look guilty. Actually, he didn't know why he should feel guilty. He had had no idea that Douglas Ward was in love with Linda McCall, and Linda certainly didn't say anything about it.

"I'm worried that he's going to do something very foolish," Nancy said.

"I'll keep an eye on him while I'm in town."

"I hate to ask it of you, after all you've done."

Clint put up his hand and said, "Don't worry about it, Nancy."

"Do you know how much longer you'll be in town?" she asked.

"Most likely no more than a couple of days," Clint said. "Maybe whatever is bothering him will take care of itself by then."

"Even after you're gone Linda McCall will still be here. She's my brother's biggest problem."

"Have you ever talked to her about him?"

"No," she said, a little too quickly. Clint felt that Nancy could not have been more than twenty-seven or eight, certainly not old. Could it have been that Nancy Ward was intimidated by Linda McCall's youth and beauty? The older woman was certainly lovely enough in her own right and, in some ways, even more desirable.

"Since I will probably be gone in a couple of days, do you think we could have dinner together before then?" he asked her.

"I . . . don't know," she said, hesitantly.

Nancy Ward was not accustomed to having dinner with gentlemen she had just met. Still, Clint Adams was attractive, and he had done a lot for Douglas since he'd been in town—not the least of which had been saving his life.

"Perhaps tonight?"

Nancy was about to accept when she remembered the last words her brother had spoken that morning. What could Douglas have meant by that? Maybe having dinner with Clint Adams would help her find out.

"Very well, Clint," she said. "Tonight, after I close the store."

"That's fine," he said. "I'll meet you there."

"Thanks for your help, Clint."

"It's my pleasure."

Chapter Thirteen

Later that day Sheriff Valdez showed up at the livery as Clint was locking up his rig.

"What now, Sheriff?" he asked. "Your cousin decided to press charges?"

"Brother. No, that is not it," Valdez said, and Clint breathed a sigh of relief.

"What, then?"

"You were speaking to a young man this morning at your hotel, is that not true?"

"At breakfast," Clint said, wondering what kind of trouble the young ranger had gotten himself into. "I bought him breakfast. So?"

"So," Valdez said, "the young man is dead."

Clint stopped cold in his tracks and said, "What?"

"He is dead."

"How?"

"Killed."

"How, goddamn it!"

Valdez took a hasty step backward and said, "He was stabbed in the belly."

"Who did it?"

"I do not know, señor," Valdez said. "That is why I have come to you."

"You think I did it?" Clint demanded. "You trying to blame this one on me?"

"No, señor," Valdez said, shaking his head sadly. "You are the only person I know of who spoke to the young man. I wish to know who he was."

He was a Texas Ranger, Clint said to himself, seething inside at a man named Captain McNelly, who sent a kid, wet behind the ears, into the field and expected him to come out without a scratch.

"I don't know who he was, Sheriff."

"But, señor, you bought him breakfast."

"He was hungry, and he had no money. Did you find any money on him?"

"No."

"Then he was robbed."

"How could he have been robbed if you say he had no money on him?"

Clint waved a hand in annoyance and said, "I forgot. Is there anything else I can do for you?"

"Have you seen him since this morning?"

"No."

Valdez frowned at Clint and then said, "Then I suppose that is all I need from you."

"Good."

"You seem upset."

"I didn't think I'd be seeing you again," Clint said, "and this meeting hasn't exactly been pleasant. Good-bye."

Valdez shook his head and turned to leave, muttering "gringos" under his breath.

"Valdez?"

The Sheriff turned and glared at Clint.

"Where's the body?"

"At the undertaker's."

"Okay, thanks."

Valdez seemed about to say something, then shook his head and left.

When Clint left the undertaker's, he spotted the same man across the street that he'd seen earlier outside the livery.

He was being followed. Who would have set that up except either Valdez or King Fisher? he thought. Whoever the man was working for, Clint was going to have to lose him.

He led the man into an alley, where he introduced himself by slamming the man up against a wall.

"Do you know who you're following?" he demanded of the man, who was significantly smaller than he was.

"Si, señor," the man said, wide-eyed.

"Who sent you?"

"My Patron."

"Fisher?"

The man nodded jerkily and said, "Si."

"Tell King Fisher I don't like being followed. Will you do that for me?"

"Si, señor," the man said, shaking uncontrollably.

"Thanks." Clint hit the man on the butt of the jaw, and left him lying on the ground.

Clint rode Duke to the next town and sent a telegram from there, informing Captain McNelly of the death of his man, Ranger Fricke, and informing him that he, Clint Adams, would find out who killed the man and dump him in McNelly's lap.

What he didn't include in the telegram was that he was going to knock McNelly on his ass directly afterwards.

"What do you mean he got away from you?" Carlos DeJesus demanded.

"He hit me," the man replied, "on the jaw and knocked me out."

"When I tell the patron that you let Clint Adams get away from you, you will wish you had never got up. Did you look around town for him?"

"Si? I even checked the livery stable. His wagon was still there, but not his horse."

"Then he left town, but he is planning to come back."

"Do you wish me to go back to town and wait?"

"No, I will send someone else. He has seen you. Go back to work."

"What will you tell the patron?"

"Do not worry. I will take care of it."

As the man walked away Carlos wondered to himself: if Clint Adams returned, why was there any need at all to tell the patron that he left? Especially after the farce with the young gringo being killed, but he had brought that on himself by grabbing Perez, the man who had been tailing him. Perez was a blade man, and he had reacted instinctively. Now Carlos knew that he should have had Perez watching the Gunsmith, and someone else watching the blond man. The error was his, but why admit it to his boss if he didn't have to?

Perhaps Clint Adams merely wished to exercise his horse.

He would wait and see.

When the Gunsmith returned to Eagle Pass it was with a new purpose in mind. He put Duke back up at the livery and went to the saloon for a drink.

His original purpose had been to wait a couple of days for King Fisher to make his move, then leave, one way or another.

Now, over a shot of hard whiskey, he swore that if King Fisher had anything to do with the dead Ranger—hell, the dead *kid*—then he would pin it on him and hand him over to McNelly.

But McNelly had some paying to do as well, for sending a kid like that after King Fisher when he should have kept him close to home base.

King Fisher, Texas Rangers, McNelly.

Shit.

Chapter Fourteen

The next morning Clint woke up and knew what he had to do. Fisher had put another man on him. He had spotted him the night before, while returning to his hotel.

After breakfast he left the hotel through a rear window, crossed the street, and came up behind King Fisher's man.

"Don't move," he said, the man stiffening at the sound of his voice. This one was bigger and older than the other one, probably meaner—but right now he was just as scared as the other one had been.

"Señor?"

"Where's your horse?"

"There, señor," the man said, jerking his chin towards the sorrel that was secured to a hitching post.

"All right. Take him and walk him to the livery. We're going for a ride."

"To where, señor?"

"To King Fisher's ranch."

"The Pendencia?"

"If that's what it's called. Move."

"You will kill me if I do not?"

"Right here, amigo."

"You leave me no choice."

They walked to the livery, where Clint kept a watchful eye on the man while saddling Duke.

Once mounted, Clint said, "All right, amigo. Lead the way."

When Clint Adams rode into the clearing in front of King Fisher's house, led by one of Fisher's own men, the rancher's vaqueros stared—including Carlos De-Jesus. The foreman quickly threw off his surprise and approached the Gunsmith.

"Can I help you?" he asked, casting a murderous glare at his man Hererra. The man looked back at Clint, who simply nodded to him and allowed him to ride off.

"I'd like to see King Fisher," Clint announced.

"I am the foreman of Pendencia."

"That's fine, but I want to see Fisher. Tell him Clint Adams is here."

"I will see if he will admit you."

"No," Clint said, "out here."

"I will ask him. You will wait, *por favor*."

The foreman disappeared inside the impressive wood-and-adobe house. While he was gone the vaqueros slowly formed a circle around the Gunsmith until he was virtually surrounded.

When Fisher appeared he called out something in Spanish, and the vaqueros reluctantly backed away.

"Can I help you, Mr. Adams?" Fisher asked from his porch. "Have you decided to accept my offer?"

"No."

"Would you like to come inside for a drink?"

"What I have to say I can say from here."

"Very well, then say it."

"A young man was killed in town yesterday."

"I heard. Tragic."

"I'll tell you something even more tragic. That young man was a Texas Ranger."

The Gunsmith was watching Fisher's eyes as he spoke, and noticed the flicker of surprise there before the man was able to mask it.

"Is that a fact?"

"Yes, it is a fact, and one that I thought you should be made aware of."

"I appreciate that."

"Here's something else you won't appreciate. I'm not leaving town until I find out who killed that boy, and if I find out it was you I'm going to hog-tie you and deliver you to the Ranger Captain McNelly myself. You know Captain McNelly, don't you?"

From the fleeting look of anxiety on Fisher's face he knew he'd hit a nerve.

"That sounds like a threat."

"The people in town were right," Clint said, bringing Duke's head around to leave. "You are smart. *Adios*—for now."

As Clint Adams rode off Carlos DeJesus moved over next to his boss.

"Shall I get my rifle, Patron?"

"Hell no, Carlos," Fisher said. "That gent just about challenged me, and I intend to accept. Have you ever known me to back away from a challenge?"

"No, Patron."

King Fisher turned to reenter the house, then stopped and faced his foreman again.

"Carlos."

"Si, Patron."

"You really want to use that rifle of yours?"

"Si, Patron."

"Then use it on the vaquero who killed that Ranger."

"Patron, he is one of your men."

"I don't care whose man he is," Fisher said. "I didn't tell him to kill anyone, did I?"

"No, Patron."

"Did you?"

"*No*, Patron," Carlos replied hastily.

"Then do it."

Carlos nodded and said, "Si, Patron. Consider it done."

Chapter Fifteen

When Clint got back to town this time he went to the general store instead of the hotel. On his way back from Fisher's ranch he suddenly remembered that he'd had a dinner engagement the day before with Nancy Ward. He hoped she wouldn't be too angry that he'd missed it.

"Hello," he said, finding her behind the counter.

She looked up and said, "Oh," when she saw him. "You're a little late, aren't you?"

"I'm afraid so, but I think I've got a good excuse."

"Really? And you'd like to explain it to me now?"

"No, over dinner tonight."

"Dinner? Tonight?"

"If you'll forgive me until then—temporarily, that is, until you hear my excuse."

"I don't like excuses," she said, "but if you'll promise me an explanation, I'll say yes."

"All right," he said. "I promise. Shall I meet you here?"

"Why not?"

75

"Thank you for understanding, Nancy."

"I don't understand anything yet."

"You will, I promise."

After that he went to the sheriff's office to talk to Valdez.

"Sheriff, there's something I think you should know about that man that was killed?"

"The young gringo?"

"Yes. He was a Texas Ranger?"

"Is that true? A Texas Ranger?"

"It's true."

"But he was so young."

"Yes," Clint said, "I know."

"How did you discover this?"

"He told me?"

Valdez frowned and then said, "You knew this when we spoke last?"

"Yes?"

"Why did you not tell me then?"

"I . . . wasn't sure, actually, but I've checked it out since then and found that he was telling the truth."

"This is terrible," Valdez said, shaking his head. "A Texas Ranger killed in my town. I will have to get in touch with them."

"His commanding officer was a Captain McNelly."

"You checked very thoroughly."

"I tried."

"Tell me, Señor Adams, when do you plan to leave our town?"

"Well, to tell you the truth, Sheriff, my plans keep changing from moment to moment, but I'll be sure to keep you informed."

"I would appreciate that."

"Sure, Sheriff."

The Gunsmith had not really decided what all of his moves would be, but he felt that he had at least planted some seeds. A lot would depend on whether or not Valdez was just a puppet of King Fisher, and on how much respect Fisher had for Captain McNelly. He would have to wait and see.

Chapter Sixteen

Nancy Ward was a totally different kind of woman than Linda McCall . . . but the net results of their dinner were the same.

They ended up in Clint Adams' room, making love.

The route there had been similar: dinner, intelligent conversation and raw passion.

In Linda McCall, her raw passion was on the surface, plain for anyone with educated eyes to see. In Nancy Ward, her desires bubbled beneath the surface where she had kept them hidden for years. It took a man like Clint Adams to bring them to the top.

"I never expected to end up here," she said as they lay in his bed together.

"I did," he said, kissing her.

"You planned this?"

"No, but I expected it."

"How modest you are."

"I don't have time for that," he said, sliding his

hand between her legs, his fingers stroking her moist cleft.

"Oh," she said, lifting her hips.

"I'm going to go slowly, Nancy," he told her, probing with one finger delicately.

"Yes," she said, breathlessly.

"I want you to remember this."

"Oh, yes," she said, biting her lip as he wiggled his fingers about inside of her. "Oh, yes!"

He brought her to climax once, using only his fingers, and then slid down so he could use his mouth.

When his tongue slid along her wet lips she grabbed him behind the head and pushed his face against her crotch. He flicked his tongue inside her, and her hips writhed uncontrollably. When his tongue came in contact with her swollen clit she almost screamed, biting her lip to keep the noise in. When she came, she couldn't hold it any longer and shouted in ecstacy.

Still later, when his engorged cock pushed into her she laughed deep in her throat, wrapping her legs around his waist. She was happy, for the first time that she could remember in a long while. This man was incredibly good for her, but she knew that he would be gone in a matter of days.

"God," she said hoarsely as he plumbed her depths. "Faster," she said into his ear, "faster and harder, Clint. Please!"

"I told you I was going to go slow."

"I know," she said, digging her hands into his back, "but I can't stand it. Just do it to me hard and fast, Clint. Now!"

"Whatever you want, Nancy," he said. "I want to make you happy."

She gasped as he increased the speed and force of his stokes and shrieked, "God, Oh God, Clint . . ."

Afterwards, Clint walked Nancy Ward back to her home.

"You said over dinner you might not be leaving as soon as you thought," Nancy reminded him.

"That's right."

"Any particular reason for that?"

"Yes. A young man was killed here yesterday. I mean to find out who did it."

"Did you know him?"

"I met him once."

"Why is finding his killer so important to you?"

"I'm afraid I can't answer that one, Nancy," he said, which caused her to stare at him with a puzzled look on her face. "Maybe it was just his youth, and the way it was wasted."

As they reached the store, neither was aware that they were being watched from inside by Douglas Ward, who was straining to catch every word.

"Clint, I don't know quite what to say," Nancy Ward said as she prepared to go inside.

"Don't say anything, Nancy," Clint said, taking both her hands. "You're a special woman."

"Good night," she said, smiling shyly. "And thank you."

Chapter Seventeen

Nancy had no sooner locked the door than a lamp was turned up and her brother stood staring at her accusingly.

"You see," he snapped. "I told you."

"Told me what, Douglas?" she shot back. "Are you drunk again?"

"I'm not drunk."

"Then what are you talking about?"

"I'm talking about high and mighty Clint Adams thinking he can take anything he wants."

"You're talking about the man who saved your life, Douglas."

He laughed bitterly and said, "Sure, that's what he thinks gives him the right."

"What right? Douglas, I don't know what you're talking about?"

"Tell me you didn't just come from his bed? Go ahead, tell me!"

"That's none of your business."

"Well, it's my business who else he's had in his bed!"

"Douglas—"

"Ask him about Linda, and see what he tells you. As for being drunk," he said, pulling the front door open, "I'm going to go and take care of that little detail right now!" The door slammed behind him.

After Douglas had stormed out of the store, Nancy immediately went to the grain bin where she had locked away all of the guns in the store, and found that the lock had been broken. Hastily, she went through the pile of guns, but it was useless. She couldn't tell if any were missing or not, but feared that her brother had taken one.

All she could think of now was warning Clint and keeping both men alive.

She found Clint back in his room, getting ready to go to sleep.

"What is it, Nancy?"

Breathlessly, she said, "I'm afraid that Douglas has finally gotten his hands on a gun, Clint. He broke the lock where I had them locked up."

"Is one missing?"

"I don't know. I can't tell."

"All right, calm down. Go back home and wait, I'll find him."

"No, that's not what I want you to do," she said, pushing him into the room. "I want you to stay away from him."

"Why?"

"He was talking some nonsense about you and

Linda McCall. I think it's you he wants to go after with the gun."

"Oh."

Studying his face she asked, "Is it true, then? Did you have Linda up here before me?"

"Nancy—"

"Oh, never mind that," she said suddenly. "It doesn't really matter. All that matters is that you and Douglas stay away from each other, otherwise one of you might end up dead. Promise me you'll try to stay away from him."

"All right, Nancy. I promise."

"I don't want either one of you to get killed."

"I'll do my best."

Nodding, she said, "All right."

"Where is he now?"

"He said he was going out to get drunk."

"He could get himself into trouble."

"You saved him once, Clint. Let him fight his own battles for a change. I just don't want it to be you who . . . who kills him."

"Nancy, about Linda—"

"I said that doesn't matter," she said, holding up her hands and closing her eyes, as if that would keep her from hearing what he had to say. "Maybe later, but right now I don't want to hear it."

"Whatever you say."

"I'll say good night, now."

"Let me know tomorrow what happens with Douglas."

"I'll keep you informed. Maybe the best thing would be for you to leave town."

"I wish I could, Nancy, but it's just not possible at this time."

"I understand. Good night, Clint."

"Good night."

He moved to his window which overlooked the street, and watched her walk back to her store. Studying the doorways across the street, all of which were darkened, he couldn't tell whether or not Ward was there. But if he was, he was better off there than inside the hotel.

As if he didn't have enough trouble, now he had to stay away from Ward in order to keep from killing him.

A shiver ran up and down his spine as he thought of Bill Hickok and Jack McCall. McCall was no gunman, but he had gotten behind Hickok and shot him in the back.

Promise or no promise to Nancy Ward, he would take no chance of that happening to him.

Across the street, in one of those darkened doorways, Douglas watched his sister walk towards home. He had a Navy Colt stashed in his belt, and a bottle of whiskey in his hand.

He stared across at the Gunsmith's hotel and knew that he wasn't drunk enough to cross that street. Not yet.

Chapter Eighteen

The next morning over breakfast the Gunsmith had to put his various problems in perspective.

His major problem was, of course, watching out for the reprisals of King Fisher and his men.

Number two on his list was finding the killer of young Ranger Fricke.

Third was Douglas Ward who, if he got drunk enough, just might come after him with a gun, getting himself killed in the process.

Then there were the feelings of both Linda McCall and Nancy Ward. Although the younger of the two, Linda was the one who would probably be more understanding, because she was basically after the same thing he was. Nancy was a different kind of woman and had obviously not a great deal of experience with sex for pleasure only. Still, staying alive had to take precedence over all else.

After breakfast he went to the livery to dispense with whatever commitments he had left in his rig. There were still two guns he had to work on and return, and then he would close up shop as far as the gunsmithing business was concerned.

It was while he was inside his rig that Sheriff Valdez showed up once again.

"What is it this time?" Clint asked when the lawman made his presence known.

"Another dead man," Valdez said, glumly. "One of King Fisher's men; a man named Hererra."

"Why come to me?"

"You were seen with him yesterday."

"Hererra?" Clint asked, repeating the unfamiliar name. Then it struck him. "A large man, scarred face?"

"That is him."

"He was watching me, and I had him take me to King Fisher's ranch."

"You went to the Pendencia yesterday?"

"If that's what it's called. How was he killed?"

"Shot in the back by someone with a rifle."

Again the shiver down Clint's back as he thought of his friend Hickok.

"I didn't kill him."

"I believe you."

"Then why are you here?"

"It is my job, señor," Valdez said. "You of all people should understand that."

"Yes."

"So, señor, I am also here asking for your help."

"My help?"

"Si. I have no deputy, and I am not experienced in these matters."

Clint studied the lawman's face and then made a snap decision.

"All right, Sheriff, I'll help you—"

"Gracias, señor."

"—as long as you answer one question for me truthfully," Clint went on.

Valdez frowned and asked, "And what question is that?"

"Are you a real sheriff, or do you work for King Fisher?"

Valdez's face turned red and for a moment Clint thought the man was going to try to hit him.

"Señor, I will allow you that question since you know that my brother works for Señor Fisher, but I will only tell you that I take my job very seriously. It will be up to you to believe me or not."

The two men exchanged glances then and Clint finally said, "I believe you."

"You will help me? You will be my deputy?"

"Whoa, I didn't say that!" Clint said, holding up both hands palms out. "I said I'd help you, but I won't wear a badge."

Valdez was obviously puzzled by the Gunsmith's attitude but he said, "Very well."

"And sheriff, let's keep this between you and me, all right?"

"As you wish, señor. Gracias."

"I'll keep in contact with you."

Valdez thanked him again and left.

Clint had to admit that knowing Valdez was a true lawman and not a puppet was something of a comfort, but how much help the man would actually be against John King Fisher was something only time would tell.

Chapter Nineteen

When Clint entered the saloon the first thing he noticed was the man sitting on the floor with his back against the bar and a bottle of whiskey in his hand.

"Who's that?" he asked the bartender.

The man shrugged and said, "A stranger."

Clint looked the man over again and said, "That's not the way to make an impression in a strange town." He turned his attention back to the bartender and said, "Give me a beer."

"Si, señor. *Cerveza*."

The bartender put a mug of beer on the bar and then walked to the other end to take care of another customer.

"Adams."

Clint looked around to see who had called his name, then shrugged and returned to his beer.

"Adams!"

This time the name came out in a desperate hiss,

wanting to be heard, yet not wanting to. It took a moment, but then Clint realized that the only man near him was the one on the floor practically at his face.

Without looking up, the man said, "Yeah, I called you. Don't look down, just listen."

Clint stared into his beer. Whoever the man was, he was lucky it was still early and the saloon was empty.

"I was sent by Captain McNelly."

"That bastard!"

"You know the captain?"

"No."

"Listen, I'm here to let you know that the captain has men poised to come riding in at a moment's notice, as soon as you come up with something on Fisher."

"You tell your captain that if he knows what's good for him he'd better not be among them."

"In any case, I'll be around. My name's Denson."

"How old are you, Denson?"

"What?" the man asked, obviously not sure he'd heard the question right.

"How old are you?"

"Shit, I'm forty-five. What's that got to do with anything?"

"A lot," Clint said. "Where will you be if I need you?"

"I'll be right behind you, friend," Denson said, "watching your back."

The Gunsmith left the saloon without getting a clear look at Denson, but he was sure he'd recognize him again when he needed him—especially if he was going to be watching his back.

Adams knew that the sheriff was on his side, and he

had a Texas Ranger watching his back. That still put the three of them against King Fisher and his many vaqueros.

Well, maybe the Ranger could at least keep Douglas Ward away from him.

Chapter Twenty

Clint went over to the undertaker's again, where he had previously viewed the body of Cliff Fricke. This time he wanted to see the body of the dead Mexican, Hererra.

The undertaker, a man named Crumley, asked Clint, "You got an interest in dead bodies in general or these two in particular?"

"These two," Clint said. "I'm working with Sheriff Valdez."

"Oh. All right, come on in the back."

Crumley took Clint in his back room and showed him the body of Hererra. The man had been shot square in the back once, but the shot had been so well placed that one had been more than enough.

"You been in this town long?" Clint asked Crumley, who was not Mexican.

"Most of my life," the white-haired man replied. Crumley was sixty if he was a day, but he carried it well.

"Who do you know hereabouts who can shoot a rifle

well enough to pierce the spade on an ace of spades?''

Crumley frowned and asked, ''You figure that's what it took to make this shot?''

''I'd be willing to bet on it.''

''A lot of men claim to be that good a shot, but I'd only bet on three or four.''

''Who?''

''Hickok, when he was alive, the Gunsmith,'' he said, obviously unaware that that was who he was talking to at the moment, ''and Warren Murphy, the Irish gun—''

''You're judging these men by their reputations.''

''I've seen Hickok and Murphy shoot,'' Crumley corrected him, ''and the Gunsmith—well, I heard Wild Bill talk about him once and, liar that Bill was, I believed him about this feller.''

''Who's the fourth man you mentioned.''

''That's a funny one. It ain't somebody you ever heard of. It's a feller who lives hereabouts and shoots damn good. I don't know if he's that good, but you asked me for someone in this area, and this here feller's the only one I can think of who might be that good.''

''And who would that be?''

''The foreman out at the Pendencia,'' Crumley answered, ''Some people 'round here call him Dead Shot, but his name's Carlos DeJesus.''

Adams paused for a moment, then looked back at the dead man.

''Where are this man's belongings? Did the sheriff take them?''

''Nah, they're here,'' Crumley said. He led Clint to another table where a pile of clothing and other personal items lay.

Clint sifted through the dead man's clothing and weapons and noticed that there was no money among the belongings. Well, maybe Crumley deserved it.

When he found the man's knife he picked it up and showed it to Crumley.

"Could this have killed the other man?"

"The lad?" Crumley asked, squinting at the blade in the Gunsmith's hand. "I'd say that was damn close to the size of the blade that killed him.

"I'm going to take this."

"I don't know if I can let you do that—"

"And we won't say anything to the sheriff about the fact that Hererra had no money on him at the time of his death."

Crumley paused and then said, "Well, seeing as how you're helping the sheriff . . ."

"I'll tell him of your cooperation."

"Let me understand this," Valdez said. "You're saying that Hererra must have killed the young Ranger, and for that King Fisher had him killed. His own man?"

"I doubt that Fisher told him to kill anyone," Clint said. "What I figure is that Hererra was watching Fricke, and the kid caught on and confronted him. Hererra panicked and killed him. When Fisher found out, he had Hererra put out of the way."

"By who?"

"Who do they call Dead Shot around here?"

"DeJesus," Valdez said, "Carlos DeJesus, foreman at the Pendencia."

"Hererra was found where?"

"On the trail into town?"

"Shot from a distance, I'd say. Otherwise he would have seen his killer and been warned."

Valdez thought it over, then said, "It makes sense."

"Of course it does."

"What can I do, then? Go out to the Pendencia and arrest Carlos DeJesus?"

"You don't have enough evidence to do that yet, Sheriff," Clint explained.

"Then what can I do?"

"Nothing, for the moment. Let me plant a few more seeds and see what pops up."

"As you wish," Valdez said, doubtfully. "Since I requested your help, I suppose I should be guided by your word."

"What you might do," Clint said after a moment, "is ride out to Fisher's ranch and simply ask a few questions, as if you were looking into Hererra's death."

"What purpose will that serve?" Valdez asked. "They will not tell me anything."

"Maybe not, but let's just blow some smoke," Clint explained. "Let Fisher think that he's successfully covered his tracks."

"And then perhaps he will become careless?" Valdez said, getting into the spirit of it.

"Exactly."

The sheriff drew himself up and said, "I will ride out there immediately. Perhaps I am not King Fisher's puppet, but I have not exactly stood up to him either. This will give me the opportunity."

Clint stopped at the door and said, "Sheriff, don't get any ideas. Just ask a couple of questions and leave. Understand?"

"Of course I understand," Valdez snapped. "Do I look like a child to you?"

"No," Clint said. "Just don't get carried away. I'll be in touch."

Clint left the sheriff's office, hoping that Valdez would take his advice.

Chapter Twenty-One

Sheriff Valdez may not have gone too far, but he did arouse some curiosity out at the Pendencia.

"What do you suppose that was all about?" Fisher asked DeJesus as Valdez rode away.

"Suddenly he is making noises like a real sheriff," DeJesus said.

"He's been talking to someone."

"Who?"

King Fisher looked at his foreman and said, "Who else? The Gunsmith."

"You think they are working together?"

"Maybe, but what I'm more concerned about is what they're working on," the flamboyant rancher said.

"Adams mentioned Captain McNelly. Perhaps they are working with him also."

"Perhaps."

"We could have the sheriff's brother speak to him."

"Is Valdez back?" Fisher asked, referring to the lawman's brother.

"He's back, but not ready to do any serious work."

"All right, then have him talk to his brother, but if he isn't able to convince the sheriff to melt away into the background we will have to take appropriate action of our own."

"Kill the sheriff?"

"No," Fisher said, rubbing his jaw. "I think that maybe I'll let you use your rifle one more time—on the Gunsmith."

Carlos DeJesus smiled.

"Unless I decide to do it myself," Fisher added. "I'll think it over and let you know. Go and talk to Valdez."

"As you wish."

Carlos DeJesus left the bunkhouse after talking to Rudolpho Valdez, the sheriff's brother, hoping that Fisher would decide to let him take care of Clint Adams.

Rudolpho was eager to help King Fisher because he had been good to him as a vaquero on the Pendencia.

"I can talk to my brother," Valdez said, "but he is very much his own man."

"It has not seemed so until now." Carlos said.

"Do not be fooled. My brother Ricardo is easy with the Pendencia's vaqueros when they are in town for my benefit, but do not try to push him, for he will most surely push back."

"We will see about that," Carlos said. "Speak to your brother."

"I will."

Now as he returned to the house to tell Fisher of his conversation he recognized that killing the Gunsmith would strengthen his own reputation, and he would become much more than just someone the people of the small border town of Eagle Pass called Dead Shot.

When King Fisher went back into his house he was thinking of Captain Lee McNelly. He knew the ranger captain had been after him for a long time, but had never had any evidence to use against him. Had he now recruited the Gunsmith to help him get that evidence?

Well, whether he had or not, the time had come to decide how to take care of Clint Adams once and for all.

Rudolpho Valdez sat in the bunkhouse nursing his injured shoulder and began to worry about his brother. He had warned his older brother not to take the job, that it would end up putting him at odds with King Fisher, but Ricardo never listened to anyone, not even their father.

Perhaps, he thought, he should go to town right now and talk to Ricardo. It was time to make Ricardo listen to someone else, and perhaps decide what side he himself was on.

Chapter Twenty-Two

While Sheriff Valdez was riding out to the Pendencia, Clint Adams was having a drink with Ranger Denson on the saloon floor at his feet.

"What do you need?" Denson asked.

"I want to see McNelly."

"What?" Denson asked. "That ain't what you said last time we talked."

"Last time we talked I didn't want to see him," Clint said. "Now I do. Set it up."

"All right."

Clint downed his drink and left the saloon. He wanted a face to face with McNelly. Why should the ranger captain be comfortable in his warm office while his men were underfire—and underfoot!

When Denson entered Captain McNelly's office, McNelly was seated behind his desk.

"Denson, my God, the stench!" he cried, leaning away from him.

"Thought I'd report in before I cleaned up, sir."

"Well, go ahead and report."

"Clint Adams wants a meeting with you, sir."

"Why?"

"He didn't say."

"Well, what do you think he wants?"

"I don't know, sir, except—"

"Except what? Come on, speak up, man! The quicker you finish the quicker you can take a bath."

"Well, sir, I don't think he likes you."

"We've never met."

Denson shrugged and said, "Maybe he wants to tell you himself."

"Denson, go take a bath. You know, sometimes I think you enjoy this disguise."

"What disguise is that, sir?"

McNelly sat behind his desk after Denson left and wondered what was on the Gunsmith's mind? The only way he was going to find out was to meet with the man. He started coughing, then brought his handkerchief up to his mouth and spit out a wad of bloody phlegm.

Hell, a ride on horseback couldn't do him any harm. He couldn't be any worse off than he was now.

When Denson returned to town he took up his position at the base of the bar, and eventually, the Gunsmith came in for another drink.

"Your meeting is set up."

"Where and when."

"Tomorrow at sunup. There's a clearing a couple of miles south of town. The Captain will be waiting there."

"Good. I'm looking forward to it."

"You puzzle me, Adams."

"Yeah?" Clint said, putting down his empty mug. "I don't think I'll puzzle your captain though."

"No?"

"No, I intend to lay it right on the line for him."

Clint dropped a silver dollar into his lap and walked out. Denson picked up the dollar, tucked it away in his pocket and said to himself, "That's one meeting I'd like to witness."

Chapter Twenty-Three

When Clint went back to his room, he did so with intentions of going to sleep, but found Linda McCall in his bed instead.

"Well, hello," she said, smiling broadly, holding the sheet up to her neck. "You keep late hours."

"Sometimes."

"I'm glad you're back."

"In a way, I'm glad you're here."

"In a way?" she asked, dropping the sheet top to her waist. Her breasts were perfectly formed, firm and round, beautiful—but at the moment he had other things on his mind.

He walked to the bed, sat beside her and pulled the sheet back up to her throat.

"We have to talk."

"What about?" she asked, taking hold of the sheet again. "If you're worried that I'll become a clinging female when it's time for you to leave—"

"That's not it."

"Then what do you want to talk about?"

"Douglas Ward."

"Douglas? Why should we talk about him?"

"Well, from what I understand, he's in love with you."

"So?"

"You know that?"

"Of course I know that. I'm the one he's been mooning around since I was fourteen."

"And how do you feel about him?"

"I don't understand what this is about?"

"Humor me."

She gave him a resigned look and said, "Sometimes I'm flattered that he hangs around me, and sometimes I wish he'd hang around somebody else."

"You're not in love with him?"

"No."

"You've never told him that you were?"

"No!"

"But you haven't told him that you're not."

She hesitated, then said, "No. What's this all about, Clint? I didn't come up here to talk about Douglas Ward."

"He's been drinking a lot lately, and his sister says he's been looking for a gun."

"What for? To shoot off his own foot?"

"I think he wants to shoot me."

"You? Why in the world would he want to do a fool thing like that? If he goes near you with a gun, he'll get killed."

"I don't have any intention of killing him," Clint said, "but I don't want him to kill me either."

"Well, why do you think he wants to?"

"Because of you."

"Me?"

"He's jealous. The other night after I walked you home I found him in a doorway across the street, drunk."

"What was he doing there?"

"I'd say he was watching us. He watched us go in, and he waited for us to come out."

"And now he's jealous enough to want to kill you?"

"That's the way it looks."

"You're not going to send me away because of that, are you?" she asked, dropping the sheet so he could see her breasts again.

"Well, if you had said something like you were engaged or something, I would."

"I'm not engaged, Clint," she said, putting her hands on his shoulders, "and I have no intentions of becoming engaged in the near future."

She pulled him toward her, raising up on her knees so that she could press her firm breasts against his face. Her already distended nipples rubbed against his chin, and he opened his mouth to take first one between his teeth, and then the other. She moaned and worked on removing his clothes.

He pulled the sheet away so that her entire body was exposed, and then began to explore it with his tongue, finding places to make her feel good that she had never even known she had. Eventually, his mouth came to a rest between her legs, and he lapped at her until her spasms shook the entire bed, and she begged him to stop.

''Please, Clint,'' she moaned, ''put it in me now. I need it now!''

He hovered over her and she reached between his legs to grasp his hard column of flesh and pull it towards her wet, waiting portal.

''Oh God, yes, that's it,'' she said as he drove into her up to the hilt. Her insides were like hot butter, and he started churning.

''Ooh, Clint . . .'' she groaned, ''slide your hands under me. I love it when you hold me like that.''

He slid his hands beneath her and took hold of her firm cheeks. Pulling her tightly against him he continued to churn her inside, taking her in hard, deep strokes until her breath came raggedly in his ear.

''Oh, Oh, Ohhh,'' she cried, and then she was bucking and writhing beneath him like a wild filly. He held her tightly by her buttocks and continued pounding into her until she was crying out incoherently for him to stop and work faster.

When he started spurting his hot semen inside her, there was no way in hell he could have understood what she was trying to say, so he stopped trying and just enjoyed himself.

''What's the matter?'' he asked later from bed as she stood wrapped in a sheet looking out his window.

''I was just looking across the street,'' she said, ''thinking about Douglas. I never meant for him to fall in love with me. And I would find it very hard to be cruel to him.''

''You don't have to be cruel to him. Just explain the situation to him.''

She turned and looked at Clint, gnawing on the nail

of the little finger of her left hand while the right hand held the sheet.

"You don't understand," she said. "With Douglas the slightest word can be like a slap in the face."

"You know him that well?"

"I didn't think I did," she said, "but he has been hanging around me for five years. I guess I learned a few things about him during that time."

"You'll talk to him?"

"Yes," she said, "I'll talk to him. But right now," she added, pulling the sheet open and dropping it to the floor, "I'd much rather talk to you."

When Clint walked Linda home she was nervous. She wanted to check the doorways, but he talked her out of it.

At her door she said, "I keep waiting for a bullet."

"No bullets, Linda," he said, taking her by the shoulders. "Talk to Douglas tomorrow. Tell him the way it is. Make him understand."

"I'll try," she said. "I'll really try."

"I know you will."

They kissed, softly at first and then with more intensity. She went inside, and he walked back toward his hotel.

He found Douglas in the same doorway as last time, with a gun in one hand and an empty whiskey bottle in the other.

"Well, at least I know where you are," he said, staring down at the unconscious, snoring man. Bending over, he picked up the gun and said, "I'll just relieve you of this and let you sleep it off right where you are, Doug boy."

He tucked the gun into his belt and again wondered if

he should take the man home or leave him where he was. In the end he simply moved Douglas around so that his legs weren't sprawled across the walk, and said, ''Good night.''

Chapter Twenty-Four

Sunup found Clint Adams awaiting the arrival of Texas Ranger Captain Lee McNelly. He didn't know exactly what he was going to say to the man, but he was smugly pleased with himself for getting a Ranger Captain out from behind his desk and on horseback so early in the morning.

He was getting restless when he heard the sound of an approaching horse. A horse and rider came into view. He was tall, and appeared older than Clint had expected. Looking at the man Clint couldn't help feeling that there was something seriously wrong with him. He was pale, and his eyes were curiously sunken into his face. He was dressed in plain trail clothes.

"Adams," the man said, reining his horse in across from Clint.

"McNelly?"

McNelly nodded and said, "I recognize you from Fort Sills on the Staked Plains."*

"That was four or five years ago."

*The Gunsmith #8: Quanah's Revenge

115

"I remember. We didn't meet, but I was impressed with you."

"I'm flattered."

"You're also angry," the man began, but he was stopped by a cough he tried to contain behind a handkerchief. It took some time but he got it under control and said, "Excuse me."

"Are you all right?"

"I'm fine," the man assured him. "Tell me, Adams, what is making you so angry?"

"Cliff Fricke."

The man nodded and said, "I thought as much."

"How could you send a kid like that in after King Fisher?" Clint demanded.

"Believe me, Adams, if I had someone else to send, I would have. I agonized over the decision for sometime, but in the end the decision made itself. I had to send someone in to contact you."

"He did that. You should have told him to get out as soon as he did."

"Those were his orders," McNelly said. "Contact you and then come back to me with your answer. I did not tell him to stay in town. That was his own idea."

Clint was about to speak, but another cough interrupted the conversation, and he waited until McNelly had survived it.

"All right, so maybe I've been angry at you for something that wasn't your fault," he admitted. "Still, he was too young to trust."

"I agree. His ambition got in the way, and I am truly sorry that he is dead. I understand from Denson that the man who killed him has been found dead himself?"

"There's a good chance that's true, but King Fisher

is still the man behind it. I'll help you get Fisher for that kid. That's my only reason, McNelly.''

''If you say so, Adams. I really don't care what your reason is, as long as you help.''

''I'll stay in contact with you through Denson.''

''That'll be fine.''

The ranger captain successfully supressed another cough and then said in a choked voice, ''Good luck.''

''To both of us,'' Clint said, as the man went into another coughing fit. Somehow he felt that the captain needed it much more than he did.

Chapter Twenty-Five

Later that morning Sheriff Valdez showed up at the hotel dining room while Clint was having breakfast. Clint knew the chances were one in a thousand that the man could have been looking for someone else.

"Not during my first meal of the day, Sheriff, please," he said, plaintively. "No bodies this early in the day."

"No bodies, señor, dead or otherwise," the sheriff said, "I assure you."

"In that case, pull up a chair and have a cup of coffee," Clint invited.

"Gracias," Sheriff Valdez said, sinking into the other chair wearily.

He signaled the waiter for a second cup and then poured the coffee for the lawman.

"What's on your mind this early in the morning?" Clint asked.

"My brother, Rudolpho—"

"The one I shot?"

"Yes. He came to talk to me. That is, he was sent to talk to me."

"By Fisher?"

"By DeJesus."

"What did you talk about?"

"Well, they wanted my brother to talk to me about staying out of the way. It was very vague about whose way I should stay out of, but my brother—urged me to stay away from you."

"Because Fisher owes me for shooting three of his vaqueros?"

"Again, it all was very vague. They also would like me to stop making noises like a real lawman."

"Your brother wasn't very helpful, was he?"

Valdez stiffened visibly and said, "My brother is afraid of King Fisher. It took great courage on his part to come to tell me that if I chose to stand with you, he would stand with me."

Clint hesitated a moment then said, "I apologize. Your brother is a brave man."

"Yes," Valdez said, standing up, "and soon we will find out if I am as well."

The sheriff had a new decision to make, Clint realized. He had been willing to go along with Clint while only his own life was in danger, but now he had to decide if he would be willing to risk his own brother's life as well.

If Valdez decided not to support him, the Gunsmith was back to square one, standing out there all alone with only a Texas Ranger who played a drunk a little too well not to be drawing from personal experience.

·   ·   ·

"Valdez back from talking to his brother?" King Fisher asked DeJesus.

"Not yet."

"Maybe he wasn't the man to send," Fisher said, rubbing the side of his jaw.

"I warned you about hiring the sheriff's brother."

Fisher gave DeJesus a quick look, and the foreman looked away.

"I know you did, Carlos," King Fisher said, "and perhaps you were right. Perhaps I'll let you rectify the error."

Chapter Twenty-Six

Rudolpho Valdez was riding back to the Pendencia, but only to pick up his belongings and draw his pay. He had decided to leave King Fisher's employ to become his brother's deputy.

Only his brother didn't know it yet.

Carlos DeJesus waited atop a ridge for Rudolpho Valdez to return by the main road. His instructions were to kill the man, but not to shoot him in the back. The death had to look like an accident, as if the man's wound had somehow caused an accident.

Still, he could make use of his rifle, his prize possession, an excellently cared for Winchester '73. He caressed the weapon until Valdez finally came into view, then sighted down the barrel and held his breath.

The body was found later in the day by an itinerant peddler who was thoughtful enough to bring the body into town rather than stripping it where it lay. Clint heard about it in the saloon and found the sheriff standing over his brother's body in Crumley's office.

"Sheriff."

Valdez turned, acknowledged the Gunsmith's presence, then looked down at his brother again.

"Apparently something spooked his horse, and with his wounded shoulder he couldn't hold on," Crumley said. "He fell off and struck his head on a rock." Sheriff Valdez turned quickly to look at Crumley and the old undertaker added, "Apparently."

"Yes, apparently," Valdez said. "Take good care of him, Crumley."

"Of course, Sheriff."

Valdez turned to Clint and motioned for him to follow him outside.

"I'm sorry," Clint said outside. "I feel responsible, in part."

"Do not," Valdez told him. "This was not an accident."

"Why do you say that?"

"I feel it."

Clint understood a lawman's instinct, and although Valdez had only been a lawman for a short time, his instinct was developing.

"All right, I respect that."

"There is no question now that I will stand with you against King Fisher."

"You think Fisher is behind your brother's death?"

"It would be too much of a coincidence to be otherwise."

"Yet, we still don't have any evidence."

"That is a problem we will have to overcome."

"And there might be a way."

"How?"

"Me."

"I do not understand."

"Fisher has to make a move against me for the incident that started all of this."

"Shooting his vaqueros."

"Right. As long as I'm in town he's got time to set something up."

"What do you mean, set something up?"

"Well, I believe that Fisher hasn't made a move against me because he hasn't found someone who would do it."

"Why not do it himself?"

"Because he'd be setting himself up for Captain McNelly. He'd be giving the Rangers something to work with, even if it's set up as a fair fight."

"What about sending DeJesus?"

"Same reasoning applies," Clint said. "Anything Carlos DeJesus does out in the open can be traced back to King Fisher."

"Why does he not just have DeJesus shoot you in the back?"

"Ah, now you have to understand men like King Fisher and myself," Clint said. "We have reputations, whether we want them or not. We have to live up to them, and we do not do that by shooting each other in the back. If he wants to kill me himself, he'll do it another way."

"Face to face?"

"I didn't say that," Clint pointed out. "No, I think someone should pass the word to King Fisher that I'm leaving town tomorrow. That way he'd have to make a move soon."

"Well," the sheriff said, stepping down off the

boardwalk, "If he comes directly at you, he will find me standing right next to you. I owe that to my brother."

"Sheriff."

"Si?"

"I still feel partially responsible for your brother's death."

"Do not," Valdez said, holding up one hand to cut the Gunsmith off. "We make our own choices in life, señor, and sometimes that choice will lead to death."

Walking away, Sheriff Ricardo Valdez had no idea of the impact that statement had on the Gunsmith.

Clint went over that statement in his mind while he lingered over a beer at a back table in the saloon. Denson was in his customary place at the base of the bar, but Clint had not spoken to him at all.

Being the Gunsmith had never been a decision that Clint Adams made willingly—but what Sheriff Valdez—a simple, border town lawman—had said made sense to him. Everyone made their own decisions, the only thing the sheriff hadn't said was that sometimes those decisions were made without them knowing it.

That meant that years ago Clint Adams had made a decision to accept the name Gunsmith, given to him by an ambitious newspaperman. What he should have done was make that newspaperman eat every one of those newspapers, but it was much too late for that now. There were other decisions to be made.

He walked back to the bar and ordered another beer, at the same time jabbing Denson in the side with the toe of his boot.

As the bartender brought him the beer he said, "Well, this could be my last beer in this place."

"Leaving?" the man asked.

Long ago Clint had learned that the most talkative man in town was usually a bartender.

"Yes, I'll be leaving tomorrow. Time to get moving again."

"Enjoy it, then," the man said, and went off to wipe down the other end of the bar.

Clint took one sip of the beer, set it down, winked at Denson, and left.

Chapter Twenty-Seven

"I heard you were leaving town tomorrow," Nancy Ward said. "I wanted to talk to you before you go. I closed the store early."

"All right," Clint said, stepping back to allow her to enter his room. It was late afternoon and Clint had gone to his room to await whatever move King Fisher was going to make.

Nancy stepped past him, and he closed the door behind her.

"How's Douglas?"

"He came home this morning looking terrible and fell right into bed. I don't know where he was. Did you see him at all?"

"No," Clint lied, "I didn't see him. Did he have a gun on him?"

"No. I guess I could be wrong about his taking one, but the lock on the grain bin was broken."

"Maybe he broke it and then changed his mind."

"I suppose that could be it."

"Is he still in bed?"

"No," she said, making a face, "he got word that Linda McCall wanted to talk to him, and he rushed right over to the bank.

"She wants to see him?" Clint said. "Isn't it usually the other way around?"

"Yes."

"Maybe this is something good."

She stared at him a few moments and when she didn't speak he asked, "What was it you wanted to talk to me about?"

She looked down at her hands and shrugged her shoulders.

"Nancy?"

"I guess . . . I guess I wanted to talk about . . . you and Linda."

With that said she looked up at him and met his eyes boldly.

"If you want to, we can talk about it."

"I don't want you to think that I . . . expect anything of you after only . . . one night," she stammered. "It's just that Douglas said something the other night that . . . that made me curious."

"There's nothing wrong with being curious, Nancy."

"I mean, Linda's young and very beautiful. If you preferred her to me—"

"Nancy," he said, moving toward her, "you're very lovely. You could compete with Linda, if that's what you wanted to do."

"But, she's so young . . ."

"And you're so old," he said, with heavy sarcasm.

She tried to smile, but it was half-hearted.

"Nancy," he said, putting his hands on her shoulders, "you're a very lovely, desirable woman. Any man in his right mind can see that."

He kissed her gently. She responded with a burning need that turned it into something much more.

When Douglas Ward walked into the bank his stomach felt as if it were filled with butterflies. This was the first time Linda had ever asked him to come around. Maybe she finally realized that she loved him.

Linda McCall saw Douglas Ward walk into the bank and wondered if she could go through with it. Telling Douglas that she didn't love him would be like kicking a helpless little dog.

"Hello, Linda," Douglas said, leaning on her teller's window ledge.

"Hi, Douglas," she said, nervously.

"You wanted to see me?" he asked eagerly.

"Uh, yes . . . yes, I did. Could you, uh, take a walk with me? I'd like to talk to you about something."

"A walk? Sure, sure we can take a walk."

The look on his face was making it even worse for her. He looked as if all of his dreams were about to come true.

"Just let me get somebody to relieve me," she said, and he nodded anxiously.

God, she hoped she could do this.

"Oh, God," Nancy cried out as Clint's warm tongue stroked her between her legs. Her hips jerked uncontrollably until finally he had to use his elbows to pin her thighs to the bed. Now that she couldn't move—he was *so* strong—the pleasure caused by his oral stimulations grew so much she hoped she could stand it without screaming.

"I don't believe you!"

Douglas Ward's face had been getting more and more red with each passing moment as Linda McCall explained the situation to him.

"You do love me!"

"No, Douglas. I'm sorry, but I don't love you. I never did, and to be perfectly honest with you, I don't think that I ever could."

"You can't mean that!"

"Douglas, please, you don't understand," she said, hurrying to explain her last statement. "I don't think I could love any man—"

"Stop it! You're lying. You're in love with Clint Adams. I've seen you with him!"

"Yes, I have been with Clint, but I don't love him."

"Well, I've got news for you," he said, ignoring her words. "He doesn't love you, because he's also been sleeping with my sister, Nancy."

"Douglas, that doesn't matter to me. Clint can sleep with anyone he wants."

"No," Douglas Ward said, "he can't, and I'm going to prove it to him."

He turned and ran off. Linda called out to him until he was out of sight.

"Oh yes, that's it, that's . . ." Nancy gasped as Clint drove the length of his rigid penis into her.

Nancy was proud of herself. She had come this far without screaming, but as he continued to take her in quick, deep strokes, she didn't know how long she would be able to last.

When Douglas Ward got to the store and found it locked, he knew that she was with Clint Adams. He went around the back to the grain bin, which still had a damaged lock, and took out a Colt revolver.

He'd show Clint Adams that he couldn't sleep with anybody he pleased to. He'd show him so he'd never forget!''

When Nancy Ward finally did scream, it had nothing to do with sensations caused by Clint Adams.

The door to Clint's room slammed open, and over Clint's shoulder, Nancy saw her brother Douglas lunge into the room with a gun in his hand.

''Wha—'' Clint said, but wasted no time. He rolled off of the naked woman, pushing her off the other side of the bed as the shot was fired.

Clint heard Nancy's cry of pain and knew that she'd been hit. He stretched for his gun, hanging in his holster on the bedpost, grabbed it and turned to face Douglas Ward. Ward saw the gun in the Gunsmith's hand and froze.

''You bastard!'' Clint shouted. He was incensed that this man had tried to shoot him in the back. He wanted to kill Douglas Ward.

He was about to pull the trigger when Nancy's moan of pain broke the spell and melted his rage.

''Drop the gun, Douglas.''

Ward didn't move.

''Drop it, damn it, or I'll kill you!''

In a convulsive movement Ward opened his hand and dropped the gun to the floor.

"You shot your sister, Douglas."

"What?"

"Go get a doctor for her, and so help me God, if you don't come back I'll hunt you down and kill you."

Ward took one step towards his sister, whispering, "Nancy, I didn't—"

"Go for the doctor!"

Clint moved around the bed to look at Nancy. She was lying on her back with blood all over her chest. Clint was unsure as to exactly where the wound was, but that amount of blood meant it had to be serious.

Chapter Twenty-Eight

"The bullet broke her collarbone on the right side," the doctor said.

"What can you do for her?" Clint asked.

"Well, it will depend on how badly off her collarbone is," the doctor explained. "If it shattered, there could be bone splinters all over the wound. Right now she's in shock."

"What about the bullet?"

"It went right through. I won't know the extent of the damage it did until I can stabilize her."

The doctor was in his fifties, a sure-handed man who Clint felt was too good for Eagle Pass.

"Have you lived here long, Doc?"

"I settled here a few years ago, Mr. Adams. The pace here is healthier for me than it was in Chicago."

"In a border town?"

The doctor grinned and said, ''You've never been to Chicago, have you?''

When Clint left the doctor's office he found a man waiting for him outside. It took a few seconds to identify him. He'd never seen Denson on his feet before.

''I remember you,'' he said. ''You're the man who's supposed to be watching my back, right?''

''I heard something happened in the hotel.''

''Something happened? Yeah, I'd say something happened, Denson. That lovesick fool Douglas Ward came damned close to putting one in my back. In my back, damn it!''

''Take it easy—''

''You take it easy. You're supposed to be watching my goddamn back, so you better damn well start doing it.''

''All right, all right,'' Denson said, deciding not to argue with a man like the Gunsmith when he was that angry. ''Consider it watched.''

Clint's jaw tensed, as if he wanted to chastise the man further, but said nothing.

''Got that out of your system?''

''Yeah.''

''Where's the girl's brother?''

''In jail—or what passes for a jail in this one-horse town.''

''And the girl? I heard she took one.''

''Yeah, she took one,'' Clint said. ''The one that was meant for me. She's inside in pretty bad shape. She's in shock. When the doc can stabilize her he'll be able to tell more.''

"I hope she makes it."

"She better make it," Clint said. "I've got enough on my conscience as it is."

Chapter Twenty-Nine

Clint walked over to the sheriff's office, where Valdez had Douglas Ward. When he walked in Douglas looked up and stared at him blankly, then lowered his head again.

"He has not said a word since we brought him here," Valdez told Clint.

"I don't wonder," Clint said, looking at Ward with disgust. He knew he should have felt some pity for a man who had just shot his own sister, but he couldn't feel anything but distaste for any man who would shoot another man in the back.

"I don't have a jail. What am I supposed to do with him? Will his sister press charges?"

"I don't know," Clint said. "I guess we'll have to wait and see if she pulls through."

"I'll press charges," Ward blurted out.

They both looked at Douglas Ward.

"What?" Valdez asked surprised.

"I said that if my sister won't press charges, I will. I deserve to be executed."

"I agree with you, Ward," Clint said, approaching the chair the man was manacled to. "I think there's nothing more despicable than a man who'd shoot another man in the back—unless it's one who'd shoot his own sister."

"I know, I know," Ward cried out, "I'm sorry, I'm so sorry." He buried his face in his hands and began to cry.

"Forget it, Ward," Clint said viciously, "you'll get no sympathy from me."

"Clint—" the sheriff said, calling the Gunsmith by his first name for the first time.

"No chance, Valdez," Clint said. "I can't feel pity for . . . for this poor excuse for a man. I've got enough problems without feeling sorry for a back-shooter!"

The Gunsmith stormed toward the door.

"Wait," Valdez said. "I still don't know what to do with him!"

"Sheriff," Clint said, opening the door to the office with great force, "use your imagination."

Outside Clint stopped and tried to rein in his temper. With King Fisher and his men floating around it wouldn't do any good to get careless. Angry men got careless—so did frightened ones.

All his life the only thing the Gunsmith had feared was being shot in the back, and now it had almost happened. At the exact moment of the shot, he had been frightened, more so than ever before in his life. Yet, if the attempt hadn't come so close to succeeding, the circumstances would be comical.

Imagine the headlines, he thought: THE GUNSMITH SHOT IN THE BACK IN BED!

And what about Nancy Ward's reputation. The only people who knew what she was really doing in his room were the two of them and her brother. Others would only be able to make assumptions.

He had to make sure that nothing got into the newspapers that would suggest what they were really doing.

He walked over to the offices of the *Eagle Pass Gazette*, to have a talk with its editor. If he gave them an exclusive story, maybe they'd print only what he told them.

Judging from his past experiences with newspapermen, he had his doubts, but it was worth a try.

"I have news, Patron."

"What kind of news, Carlos?"

"First I have heard that Clint Adams plans to leave town tomorrow."

"Tomorrow," King Fisher said. "Well, that forces my hand, doesn't it? I found a man who might have a chance against the Gunsmith, but he can't get here by tomorrow."

"Who did you find?"

"A man named Warren Murphy. They call him 'the Irish Gun.' "

"He agreed to take the job?"

"I haven't gotten a reply to my wire yet. I had one of the other men send it."

"Why?"

"I didn't want you to be disappointed—and now it looks like you won't have to be."

"You mean—"

"I mean we'll have to go after Adams between now and tomorrow morning. All we have to do is figure out how. What else was it that you wanted to tell me?''

"Someone tried to shoot him in the back today.''

"Who was it?''

''The man who runs the general store with his sister.
His name is Douglas Ward.''

"Why would Ward want to kill Adams?''

''The word in town is that Ward is in love with the
bank manager's daughter, and she has been seeing
Adams.''

"How interesting.''

"Also, Ward's sister was in Adams' room when he
tried to kill him, and he shot his own sister by mistake.''

"Is she dead?''

"Not yet. She is at the doctor's.''

"Well, it sounds like the Gunsmith has had a very
exciting day,'' Fisher said. "I'm glad Ward didn't
succeed. A bullet in the back isn't the way a man like
Adams should be killed.''

"Yes, Patron.''

"What has happened to Ward?''

"He's under arrest. I do not know what they intend
to do with him.''

"Well, I suppose that will depend on his sister,''
Fisher smiled, "and on Adams—if he lives past tomorrow.''

Chapter Thirty

Early that evening, Clint Adams walked into the saloon to find Denson, who once again was in position holding up the bottom of the bar with his back.

"What?" Denson said as Clint moved in next to him.

"Let's stop the nonsense, Denson," Clint said, looking directly at the man. "By now these people know what the story is, and we're not fooling them with this act of yours."

"Maybe not," Denson said. "But I like it down here. What's on your mind."

"What's on my mind is you taking a nighttime ride back to your headquarters and getting McNelly and a bunch of Rangers back here by morning."

"That's not a nighttime ride, my friend," Denson said, "that's an all-night ride."

"Maybe," Clint said. "But you're going to make it anyway."

"Is there any particular reason why I'm taking this

ride?'' Denson asked. ''I mean, just in case somebody should ask, like Captain McNelly.''

''As far as King Fisher knows I'm leaving this town come morning,'' Clint explained. ''That means he's got to move against me by then.''

''So I ride out and he moves against you tonight without me to watch your back.''

''If he comes into town with his *vaqueros*, I'm in big trouble—with or without you.'' Clint said. ''Besides, I don't think he'll do anything until morning.''

''Why not?''

''Because I wouldn't.''

''You saying that you and Fisher are alike?''

''In some ways. Look, my friend, how about hauling your ass up off the floor and sticking it on your saddle. The sooner you leave, the sooner you'll get back.''

Since it was at least a five hour ride each way from the border town to the town of Goliad, where McNelly and his Rangers were headquartered, Denson couldn't really argue with that.

He picked himself up off the floor, dusted himself off with little effect and faced the Gunsmith squarely.

''Just 'cause you got something eatin' at your butt, friend, don't think you can take it out on me. When this is all over maybe we should talk about it.''

''When this is all over I don't even want to be within spitting distance of a Texas Ranger. You got something to say, say it now.''

''Your reputation don't mean spit to me, Adams. You're upset 'cause you was almost shot in the back. I can understand that. I been shot at myself a time or two. But that don't mean I started biting the people who was around to help me."

They matched glares for a few seconds, and then the Gunsmith said, "You just may be right about that, Denson. I'll think about it."

"You do that. Meanwhile, I guess I'll be seeing you a little before sunup."

Denson nodded to him and left, and Clint turned to order a beer from the bartender.

"Is he coming back?" the barkeep asked.

"Maybe. Why?"

"He hasn't been good for my business."

"To tell you the truth," Clint replied, "he hasn't been very good for mine either."

When Clint left the saloon he stopped short of stepping into the street and looked around. He swept the darkened doorways with his eyes, wondering if any of King Fisher's boys might be waiting to put one in his back. Fisher himself wouldn't shoot him in the back, but who knew what his vaqueros might try to do, thinking that they were doing him a favor.

Then again, maybe he was just skiddish after the close call with Ward.

Had he been too hard on Ward? Probably, but the little bastard deserved it. Even now, after he'd calmed down a bit, he still felt his temperature rising when he thought about what Ward had tried to do.

Clint decided to stop in at the doctor's office before going back to his hotel, with a short stop at the livery to make it appear he was readying his team and rig to leave in the morning.

He stepped into the street, tensing his shoulders for the possible impact of a coward's bullet.

Chapter Thirty-One

The cowards weren't in the doorways though. They were waiting at the livery stable.

"He has to come in here to make sure that his rig is ready to go in the morning," one of King Fisher's vaqueros said to his three compadres. His name was Beniquez, and knowing that Clint Adams was giving his boss difficulty, he decided to take three of his amigos and take care of this gringo they called the Gunsmith.

"Paco," one of the other men said.

"Si?"

"This gringo—they say he is very fast with a gun."

"Don't be worried," Paco Beniquez said. "We will not give him a chance to reach his gun. We will hit him as soon as he comes through the door."

"We will shoot him in the back?"

"No," Beniquez said, "Patron would not like that, but we will teach him not to give our Patron trouble."

"And if he does not wish to learn?" another man asked.

"There are other ways that he can die," Paco said then, grinning wolfishly. "Many ways."

The doctor told Clint that there wasn't much change in Nancy Ward's condition. He also told him that was good. If she made it through the night, then there was a good chance she'd recover. What the doctor didn't know was what her physical condition would be when she fully recovered. That would depend on how badly her collarbone was damaged.

"What could happen?" Clint asked.

"One shoulder might end up lower than the other, which would give her something of a lopsided appearance."

Clint's stomach churned. She was a lovely woman, but how would she look if the collarbone didn't heal right?

He left the doctor's office feeling worse than he had in some time. He toyed with the idea of going back to the saloon for a bottle of whiskey, but decided to walk over to the livery and check out his rig and team, not to mention Duke.

He was preoccupied when he entered the livery stable, but he got his mind on business pretty damn fast when the first man hit him from behind between the shoulder blades.

"Where is Beniquez?" Carlos DeJesus asked the other men in the bunkhouse. He looked around further and noticed that there were three other men missing, three who usually spent their leisure time with Paco Beniquez.

Beniquez was looking for DeJesus' job and Carlos knew that. Beniquez also knew that King Fisher was concerned with the activities of the Gunsmith, and Paco was the type to do something stupid.

"Sanchez," he called, and a small man came running eagerly toward him. "Saddle my horse. I have to go into town—pronto!"

He hoped he wouldn't be too late.

The Gunsmith moved with the blow, hitting the ground with his shoulder and rolling. He was dimly aware that there were others in the stable, but he couldn't tell how many. It was too dark, and things were happening too fast.

He kept rolling, hoping to get away from them, but rolled right *into* one of them, knocking him off his feet.

"Paco—" the falling man cried out, but he was cut short by the Gunsmith's boot as it struck him on the side of the jaw.

"Tomas?" a voice called out.

"A light. *Cabrone*, I told you we need a light!"

A light would have warned the Gunsmith, but Paco Beniquez was starting to wish he had allowed at least one lamp to be lit.

Clint decided to turn it to his advantage. He knew the best thing he could do at the moment was remain still and not give away his position. An unconscious man was lying across his legs and he moved slowly, trying to free himself as quietly as he could.

He guessed that the first blow was supposed to put him down and make him an easy target for their boots, only he'd moved instinctively, ruining their plans.

Now they had to make new plans in the dark.

"Paco, what do we do?" a voice hissed in the darkness.

Clint eased his gun out of his holster and waited for a reply.

None came.

Paco was smart enough to keep quiet, but the other men were not as smart.

"Paco, *que pasa*?" a voice hissed. Clint pointed his gun in the direction of the voice and fired.

There was no doubt that he hit the man. He heard a sickening thud as the bullet smacked into the man solidly, and the man grunted.

That made one unconscious, and one wounded, maybe dead.

Suddenly the remaining men dashed for the doors, and he let them, not wishing to kill anyone else. He'd leave them to King Fisher, who would not appreciate their attempted ambush.

Carlos was riding into town toward the livery, when he saw Paco Beniquez and another man running out of the stable.

"Paco," he called, but the man kept running towards his horse. As he passed, Carlos saw the look of absolute terror on his face.

The other man, recognizing Carlos, paused only long enough to tell him, "The man is truly a devil. He sees in the dark."

As the man followed in Paco's wake, Carlos smiled and shook his head. Obviously, the ambush instigated by Paco Beniquez had failed, and the Gunsmith was still very much alive.

Carlos paused, eyeing the front doors of the livery and wondered how long it would take the Gunsmith to decide that it was safe to leave the structure. He could wait and . . . but no. The Patron had other plans, and it was bad enough that Beniquez and his compadres had almost ruined them.

King Fisher would be angry enough without his foreman adding to it.

DeJesus executed a small bow in the general direction of the Gunsmith, reined his horse around and headed back to the Pendencia.

"That one is one of King Fisher's men," Sheriff Valdez said, pointing to the man Clint Adams had killed, "and that one, too," he said, pointing to the other man, who only now was regaining consciousness.

"That's no surprise."

"Does this mean we have some evidence against King Fisher?" Valdez asked.

"Not at all," Clint said, rolling the dead man over onto his back so that he could see his face. "These men didn't have to be acting on Fisher's orders, and I suspect—no, damn it, I'm sure—that they weren't."

The other man staggered to his feet, and Valdez moved in and removed his gun from his holster.

"You're under arrest Sanchez."

Sanchez turned his head and peered at Clint Adams' face, using the light from the lamp Valdez had lit and hung on a wall.

"You work for Fisher, don't you?" Clint asked.

Still dazed the man admitted as much.

"Did he send you?"

The man shook his head.

"All yours, Sheriff," Clint said, and started to go for the door.

"Where are you going?"

"To my hotel to get some sleep," Clint said, "I've got a big day tomorrow."

"But now I have two prisoners and no place to keep them," Valdez complained. "What shall I do?"

"Shackle *that* one to a heavier chair," Clint suggested, and started for his hotel.

Chapter Thirty-Two

Clint approached the door to his hotel room with his gun drawn, just in case a few more of Fisher's men were left in town looking to do their boss a good turn.

There was someone in his room, but it wasn't any of Fisher's men. It was Linda McCall.

"I hope you're not going to shoot me," she said.

"No," Clint said, holstering his gun, "I've shot enough people for one day."

"What do you mean?" she asked from his bed. She had the sheets held up to her throat, and Clint noticed that they were clean. The hotel people had removed the bloody sheets, but they couldn't do anything about the holes in the headboard and the wall.

He explained what had happened in the livery while unbuckling his belt and removing his boots. She put her hands on his shoulders, letting the sheet drop to her waist.

"Do you want me to leave?"

"No," he said, turning to face her. He looked at her

bare breasts, nipples already hard, and said, "I can use the company."

"I thought you might," she said, taking his hands and placing them on her firm breasts so that her nipples scraped his palms. "I couldn't bare to think of you being alone at a time like this."

"You're a good friend, Linda."

"We are friends, aren't we?"

"Yes," he said, leaning toward her, "we definitely are."

He pushed her down so that she was lying on her back and then began to roam her body with his mouth and hands. When he touched her she felt as if she were just coming alive, like a flower opening in response to the rays of the hot sun.

When he settled down with his face between her legs she put her head back, closed her eyes and cradled his head with her hands, opening her thighs wide. His tongue darted in and out of her, licking her thoroughly before it started describing circles around her rigid clit.

"Oh, Clint . . ." she moaned.

Later they changed places, and it was Linda with her head between Clint's legs, using her tongue to moisten his pulsing cock, allowing him to slide in and out of her mouth and using her teeth and lips to bring him to the brink of exploding. She fondled his testicles in her hand, sucking on him at the same time, and suddenly he shot his juice into her eager mouth.

When he finally slid into her moist, wet cavern and pounded away at her, she wrapped her legs around him and squeezed him tightly with her strong thighs.

When they both came together it was like an earthquake. It felt as if he were ejaculating hot needles into her, and the sensation was increasing her own spasms until the pleasure was almost unbearable.

For Clint, it felt as if her insides had wrapped themselves around him like a hot, slick glove, yanking his orgasm from him greedily. Each time he felt as if he had run dry, she did something with her muscles, demanding more from him and getting it.

"What now?" she asked, wrapped up in his arms. Both of their bodies were damp with sweat and the air felt cool as it dried them.

"Sleep would be nice," he said, "but I'll have to rig the door and window just in case anyone tries to come through after you leave."

"I'm not leaving," she said, "I told you I didn't want you to be alone."

"Now, Linda—"

"We're friends, Clint," she argued, cutting him off. "You said so yourself. Friends help each other."

She adjusted her position, reached for his head, and pulled him against her.

"Sleep now," she whispered in his ear, cradling his head against the warm, damp pillows of her breasts. "I'll stay awake and keep watch for you."

"A friend," he said drowsily, "that's what you are, all right."

Chapter Thirty-Three

King Fisher's fist exploded against the jaw of Paco Beniquez, propelling the man backwards across the room before he finally hit the floor with his back.

"Draw your pay," Fisher said, "You're through."

"Patron, no—"

"I make the decisions around here, Paco," Fisher said. "You forgot that, and you cost me two men."

Fisher turned to face the other man and said, "What about you?"

"Paco said—"

"Draw your pay, too," Fisher said to the man whose name he didn't know. "Around here *I* say, and if you don't know that, you don't belong."

John King Fisher turned to Carlos DeJesus and said, "Get them both out of here and see that they're off my land before the sun comes up."

"Si, Patron," DeJesus said. "I will give them an escort."

"You do that," Fisher said, "and then come back here. We've got to decide what we're going to do tomorrow to make sure that the Gunsmith's stay in Eagle Pass will always be a memorable one.''

Captain Lee McNelly looked up as Ranger Denson entered his office.

"You didn't stop for a bath, eh?"

"No time,'' the grimy, smelly Ranger said. "Whatever is going to happen in Eagle Pass is going to happen between now and morning.''

"Who says?"

"Adams.''

"What does he want us to do?"

"Back him up.''

"That's what you were there for.''

"I didn't do such a good job,'' Denson admitted, and explained to McNelly what had occurred.

McNelly sighed. "All right, see how many men you can roust and have my horse saddled. We'll leave—'' McNelly was cut off by a cough. He put his hand to his mouth and grimaced at the brackish taste of his own blood.

"You okay, Cap'n?"

"I'm fine, Denson. Get the men together. We'll leave as soon as they're ready. I want to get there before the party starts.''

Chapter Thirty-Four

Captain McNelly had never felt worse in his life, but he owed it to Adams to be there. He was outside town with seven Rangers just before sunup. He sent Denson back into town to keep his eyes open.

"At the first sign of trouble," McNelly said, "we'll be there."

"I'll count on it," Denson said and rode back to town.

Clint left his hotel room after promising Linda McCall he wouldn't do anything foolish—which was a completely foolish thing to say.

Before going over to the sheriff's office to meet Valdez, he went to the doctor's office to check on Nancy Ward's condition.

"How is she, Doc?"

The doctor said, "She's awake. Her fever has gone down and I may be able to probe today. She's been calling for you and her brother."

"Can I see her?"

"Briefly."

Clint walked past the doctor and entered the room where Nancy was lying, her injured shoulder swathed in bandages.

"Nancy?"

Her eyes fluttered open and she turned her head painfully to look at him.

"Clint," she said in a barely audible whisper.

"How are you doing?" he asked, moving alongside the bed.

"I'll be all right," she assured him. "How is Douglas? Where is he?"

"He's all right. He's in custody."

"No," she whispered, closing her eyes.

"Nancy—"

"I don't want him in jail."

"Nancy, he shot you."

"He didn't mean to."

"No, you're right," Clint said. "He was trying to kill me."

"Clint—"

"He tried to shoot me in the back."

"Oh, Clint, he's so—he wouldn't be able to survive in jail."

She was becoming agitated, and he decided that this could be discussed another time.

"All right, Nancy, all right," he said, touching her hand. "We can talk about that when you're feeling better."

"He can't go to jail, Clint, he can't—"

"Shhh, you're going to get me in trouble with the doctor," he told her. "I have to go, but I'll be back later."

"What are you going to do?" she asked. "Where are you going?"

"I have to talk to the sheriff."

"About Douglas?"

"Among other things, yes."

She squeezed his hand with surprising strength and said, "He didn't mean it, Clint. I swear."

"Get some rest," he said, leaning over to kiss her forehead. "I'll come and see you again."

"Can I see him?"

"I'll ask the sheriff."

"Thank you."

When Clint entered the sheriff's office Douglas Ward looked up from his position, shackled against a metal link in the wall.

"Where'd you find that?" Clint asked Valdez, referring to the metal ring.

"In the livery," the sheriff said, looking up from his desk.

"Adams, you've got to listen to me," Douglas Ward called out desperately.

"No, I don't," Clint said, looking at the man with distaste. "But for your sister's sake, I will."

"How is she?"

"Doc says she's doing better."

"Thank God," he breathed. "Adams, you've got to give me a gun and let me help you."

"You're joking," Clint said. "I wouldn't give you a gun now if my life depended on it."

"But—"

"For one thing, it would be totally useless in your hand," Clint went on, "and for another, there's no telling who you might shoot—by accident, of course."

Clint ignored Ward and turned to tell Valdez, "His sister would like to see him."

"Perhaps," Valdez said, "if we are still alive this afternoon I will take him over there."

"Good point," Clint acknowledged.

At that point the door to the sheriff's office opened and Ranger Denson walked in.

"Well," Clint said, "nice to see you."

"I thought you might be pleased."

The Ranger was much cleaner than Clint had ever seen him.

"Where's McNelly?"

"Just outside of town."

"How many men has he got with him?"

"Seven."

Clint stared at the man hard, and Denson said, "Eight, if you count me."

"Oh, well," Clint said sarcastically, "then that's different."

Chapter Thirty-Five

The Pendencia vaqueros rode into town a half hour after Clint got to the sheriff's office.

"Here they come," Clint said as he looked out the window.

Valdez and Denson moved alongside Clint to look outside as well.

"Who's leading them?" Denson asked. "That's not King Fisher."

"It's DeJesus," Clint said, "the foreman. I don't see Fisher."

"This isn't the way it was supposed to happen," Denson complained.

"I'm sorry," Clint said, "I'll go out and speak to them for you."

"Señor," Valdez said, putting his hand on Clint's arm. "I am the law here. I will go out and speak to them first and see if I can get them to leave town without trouble."

"I understand, Sheriff. Go ahead. Good luck."

Valdez took a deep breath, then took a rifle off a gun rack and stepped outside.

"Where the hell is Fisher?" Denson asked aloud. It was a question Clint couldn't answer, so he just remained silent and watched Sheriff Valdez approach the large group of vaqueros.

King Fisher was busily working at the ropes that were binding his hands behind his back to the chair he was seated in.

Fisher was still shocked at the events that had taken place earlier that morning.

He was seated in his office behind his desk when Carlos DeJesus entered with three vaqueros who were apparently loyal to him.

"Carlos, what's this?" Fisher asked. The foreman did not usually enter without knocking and was always alone.

"Tie him," DeJesus said, and two of the vaqueros moved towards Fisher.

Fisher's hand flashed to his desk drawer, where he always kept a gun, but DeJesus called out, "Please don't!"

Fisher looked up and saw DeJesus pointing a gun at him.

"What's this all about, Carlos?" he demanded as the other two men pinned his arms and began to tie his hands behind his back.

"I am going to town to kill the Gunsmith," DeJesus told him.

Fisher misinterpreted his foreman's words. "Carlos, I appreciate your loyalty—"

"It is not loyalty that makes me do this, Patron,"
DeJesus said, "but ambition. *I* wish to be the man to
kill Clint Adams and make a reputation for myself."

"Carlos, you know what this means—" Fisher's
words were cut off as the man tying his hands pulled
the ropes taught.

"Si, it means I will not be working here anymore,
but then once I kill the Gunsmith, I won't have to."

The two vaqueros finished tying Fisher to his chair,
and then went back to stand by Carlos DeJesus.

"I am sorry, Patron," DeJesus said, "truly I am,
but I am afraid that my own reputation is more important to me than yours."

"You're a dead man, Carlos."

"Then I suppose I should kill you now," the ex-
foreman said, pointing his gun at Fisher's head and
cocking the hammer.

Fisher didn't flinch, and DeJesus eventually eased
the hammer down and said, "But I will not." He
holstered his gun and said to his companions, *"An-
dale."* Turning back to Fisher he said, "Good-bye,
Patron."

Now Fisher worked feverishly at the ropes that
bound him, chafing his wrists raw in his attempt to
loosen them sufficiently to free himself. He wanted to
get to town and reclaim his vaqueros from Carlos
DeJesus. He was sure that the bulk of them were loyal
to him, and that Carlos had probably lied to them in
order to get them to follow him. They would have no
reason to doubt DeJesus, since he was the foreman, but
once Fisher himself arrived, he was sure they would
turn to him.

First, however, he had to get loose.

Sheriff Valdez approached the mounted vaqueros and directed himself to Carlos DeJesus.

"I would advise you to turn around and ride back to the Pendencia."

"We could ride right over you, Valdez," DeJesus said.

"If you did that," Valdez said, staring the man right in the eye, "I would not be the first Valdez that you killed."

"I do not know what you mean," DeJesus said. "We have broken no law in Eagle Pass, Sheriff. You cannot stop me and my men from riding into town."

"No, I cannot," Valdez said, "but I can warn you that any trouble you might cause will be met with resistance."

"From you?" DeJesus asked, looking amused.

"From me."

"We have come to town for Clint Adams, Sheriff," DeJesus said, deciding to be frank. "He must be paid back for what he did to our three compadres—one of whom was your brother."

"Do not talk to me about my brother, DeJesus!"

"Very well," DeJesus said, stiffening his back at the sheriff's tone. "I would advise you not to get in the way. We only want the Gunsmith."

"Do you think you have enough men?" Valdez asked, looking past DeJesus at the twenty or so vaqueros he had with him.

"We have what we need. Don't decide to play sheriff this time, Valdez. It would not be healthy."

"I will be around, DeJesus," Valdez said. "On that you can depend."

With that Valdez turned his back and stalked back to his office.

"Where's Fisher?" Denson demanded as Valdez came back to his office.

"I do not know. DeJesus did all of the talking and seems to be in charge."

"I can't believe that Fisher sent DeJesus in for me," Clint said, shaking his head.

"He said that he is here for you, whether Fisher sent him or not," Valdez explained.

They all looked out the window and watched De-Jesus and the vaqueros ride towards the saloon. As DeJesus dismounted he barked out orders. All of the men dismounted except for five, who rode on towards the livery.

"Well, they've got the livery, the saloon, and the main street covered," Denson said, turning to face Clint, "what are you going to do?"

"I don't know, Denson," Clint said. "I really don't know."

"I don't know, Clint," Valdez said, "but it seems to me that your only chance is to get out."

"Maybe," Clint said.

"Maybe? What else can you do?"

"I can go out there in the middle of the street and call DeJesus out. Maybe he'll face me."

"And maybe they'll just all shoot you down," Denson said. "How do you expect me—us—to cover you against more than twenty guns. It's insane."

"Maybe," Clint said again. "You know, I've got a

hunch that DeJesus is here on his own.''

"On his own? He's here with twenty men!'' Denson said, incredulously.

"What I mean is that King Fisher is not behind it. I think DeJesus is after a reputation of his own and decided to beat Fisher to me. He's not going to get that reputation by having twenty men shoot me down.''

"DeJesus is very good with a rifle,'' Valdez pointed out, ''not a pistol. He will not face you fairly.''

"He's got a point there,'' Denson said, agreeing with the law man.

"You know, you fellas don't really have to get involved with this.''

"I am involved,'' Valdez said. ''My brother's murder has involved me.''

"I'm involved because it's my job,'' Denson said. ''Simple as that.''

"All right, then,'' Clint said. ''I'm walking out the front door into the street and calling for DeJesus. We'll just have to handle whatever comes after that.''

Denson and Valdez exchanged glances and then the lawman said, ''As you wish.''

"You're the boss,'' Denson added, shrugging. ''At the first sound of shots, McNelly and the Rangers are going to come riding in anyway. All we have to do is stay alive long enough for them to get here and help.''

"Then let's go,'' Clint said and opened the front door.

Just outside of town Captain Lee McNelly fidgeted in his saddle, holding his white linen handkerchief to his mouth.

"How long are we gonna wait, Cap'n?" one of the Rangers with him asked.

"We've got to wait for a signal."

"Like what?"

"Like a shot."

"But that'll probably mean the trouble's already started," the man argued.

"I know that, Harris," McNelly said. Staring in the direction of Eagle Pass, McNelly added under his breath, "I just hope they keep King Fisher alive until I get there."

King Fisher saddled his horse, ignoring his raw and bloody wrists. His only concern was getting to town before DeJesus could kill Clint Adams.

"Spread out," Clint said as they stepped into the street and crossed to the saloon. Standing on either side of him, the other two men increased the distance between them until they were all about twelve feet apart.

"DeJesus!" Clint called. "Carlos DeJesus!"

It took a few moments but DeJesus finally appeared at the front entrance of the saloon, peering out over the batwing doors.

"Señor Adams," he said, smiling pleasantly, as he stepped outside. "How nice of you to keep me from having to search for you."

"Well, I heard you were looking for me, and I thought I'd see what it was all about."

"Bueno. Then I will tell you," DeJesus said. "When you first came to town you shot three of our men, killing one and injuring the others."

"In self-defense," Clint said. "It was a fair fight. Just ask the sheriff."

"We feel it is our duty to make you pay for what happened to our compadres." As DeJesus spoke, the vaqueros began to file out the door behind him. "We have decided to make you pay with your life."

Chapter Thirty-Six

The first volley of shots drew blood, though none of the wounds were fatal.

Clint, Valdez, and Denson all began moving as the men in front of the saloon drew their weapons.

Valdez felt a bullet smack into his arm as he ran for cover.

Denson was shot in the leg.

Clint Adams felt a hot chunk of lead draw a searing line across the side of his neck as he fell behind a horse trough.

The three men began to return fire, Denson and Clint each scoring a hit with their first shot. As two of the vaqueros slumped to the ground, the others scattered for cover.

"Now what?" Denson shouted from his position behind a buckboard.

"Now we handle the situation," Clint shouted back. "Are you hit?"

"Yes, but not bad," Denson said. "So's the sheriff.

What about you?''

"Not bad.''

The firing stopped then, as suddenly as it started and they took the opportunity to eject their used shells and reload their weapons.

"If they work around behind us, or onto the rooftops, we are in trouble,'' Valdez called out to Clint in a loud rasp that was supposed to be a whisper.

Clint nodded and pointed across the street.

They all looked up and saw that some of the vaqueros were indeed working their way up to the roof of the saloon. From there they'd have access to the other rooftops. In addition, Clint wondered if the four vaqueros who were at the livery would stay there or come running over to help.

"What now?'' Denson asked.

"Where are your Rangers?''

"They're coming. Don't worry.''

Denson just hoped they would get there in time and that seven Rangers would be enough.

When the shooting stopped McNelly felt a chill up and down his spine, and urged his horse on faster. They'd be at the center of town in minutes, and he was afraid of what he would find.

The hail of lead started again, this time coming from across the street and from the rooftops. A slug nicked Valdez's earlobe. A bullet gave Denson a haircut and put him in need of a new hat. A piece of lead slid along Clint Adams' left bicep, drawing blood.

When the shooting stopped Carlos DeJesus called out from across the street, ''Stand up and make it quick for yourself, Señor Adams. It could be very painful this way."

"We're going to have to make a run for it," Clint said to Denson, who was closest to him. "Tell Valdez."

"Where are we running to?"

"Better cover."

"There ain't no such animal," Denson said. As he turned to inform Valdez of their plan, DeJesus called out an order and the shooting started again.

"Damn," Denson said, as a bullet hit his gun, tearing it from his hand and injuring his wrist.

Clint and Valdez began to fire back and then suddenly a group of men on horseback turned into the street.

"There they are!" Denson shouted.

Clint recognized McNelly leading the Rangers, all of whom had their guns draw. Unfortunately, the men on the rooftops saw them and reacted immediately. A rain of lead fell on the approaching men, knocking two from their saddles, and killing two horses. McNelly reined in and called for his men to find cover.

"Seven Rangers," Clint called out to Denson in disgust.

Denson picked up his weapon, which fortunately had not been damaged, and transferred it to his left hand. He couldn't shoot as well that way, but the way things stood, it didn't make much of a difference.

They'd be dead soon, anyway.

As King Fisher turned down the main street he saw the mounted men fall prey to the gunmen on the rooftops and watched them dismount and scatter for cover. He saw Clint Adams crouched behind a horse trough, and knew that he was in time.

"Who the hell is that?" Denson called out as he spotted a horseman coming from the other direction.

Clint looked up and said, "It's Fisher."

"Came to be in on the kill, huh?" Denson shouted out.

The men across the street also saw King Fisher and stopped firing.

Carlos DeJesus was the last person to spot King Fisher, and he cursed aloud in two languages.

"Keep firing," he shouted, standing up. *"Hijos de un Cabrone!* Keep firing!"

No amount of shouting, however, could get Fisher's vaqueros to fire while their Patron was in danger of being hit.

DeJesus looked around for the three men who had helped him tie up Fisher earlier. They were all sprawled lifeless in the dirt.

Fisher pulled his horse to a stop right between the two warring factions and called out, "All of my men withdraw. Go back to the Pendencia. Pronto!"

The men obeyed immediately, all but Carlos De-Jesus.

"Carlos," Fisher called.

DeJesus stood up, holding his rifle in his left hand.

"You wanted the Gunsmith, Carlos," Fisher said. "Well, he's all yours."

Clint holstered his gun and stood up. DeJesus eyed him, and stepped down into the street. The other vaqueros had reached street level, mounted up and began to ride back to Fisher's ranch.

McNelly and his Rangers—some of whom were

limping now—stood up and moved closer.

"He's all yours, Carlos," Fisher said again.

"Wha—"

"Your rifle against my gun, Carlos," the Gunsmith said. "What could be better?"

The look in Carlos DeJesus' eyes and on his face was one of pure fear.

"No," DeJesus cried out, throwing his rifle into the dirt, "No, don't. Señor, do not shoot!"

Denson came forward and picked up DeJesus' rifle.

"Don't worry, friend," he told DeJesus. "He won't."

At that moment McNelly rushed over to King Fisher's horse and, pointing his gun up at the man, said, "Down off your horse, Fisher. I've finally got you."

Fisher looked down at McNelly and said, "How are you, Captain."

"Never mind, just get down off your horse."

"Instead of playing games with me, Captain, I think you should get your men some medical attention."

McNelly turned and looked at his men, all of whom were wounded. One of them was clutching a bloody shoulder and leaning against a man who was bleeding from a cut on his head. Denson limped over to stand next to Clint and watch his boss in action.

"You're under arrest, Fisher," McNelly said. "When I have you behind bars, I'll take care of my men."

"Behind bars?" Fisher asked.

"Excuse me, Captain," Valdez said, stepping forward, "but we do not have a jail."

"What? No jail?"

"And no bars, I guess," Fisher said. "But that's all right, McNelly, because you've got nothing to arrest me for."

"What do you call this farce?" McNelly asked, pointing to three of Fisher's own men who were dead.

"I had nothing whatsoever to do with this," Fisher said, looking amused now that he was back in control. "It was all Carlos' idea. He did it without consulting me at all."

McNelly looked at Carlos DeJesus, who was looking down at the ground. He was feeling a gamut of emotions, not the least of which was humiliation.

"I don't—"

"It's true," Clint said, cutting McNelly off.

"What?"

"I'm afraid that's so, Cap'n," Denson said. "Look at Fisher's wrists."

McNelly looked up at Fisher's hands, which were resting on the pommel of his saddle. The man's wrists were bleeding and raw.

"Carlos must have tied you up this morning, right?" Clint asked. "He wanted to be the one to kill me and make a reputation for himself."

"That's right."

"But he worked for Fisher," McNelly said helplessly.

"McNelly, you know you can't legally hold Fisher responsible for the actions of his men. For that matter, are you going to arrest all of Fisher's vaqueros?"

"I—" McNelly began, looking around.

"You don't have enough men. All you've got—if you want something to show for all this—is his foreman, DeJesus."

"Ex-foreman," Fisher corrected. "He got fired this morning."

McNelly began to look around for some help, but there was none to be had.

"Damn it," he said under his breath. He looked around for a reasonably healthy Ranger and said, "Williams, take that man into custody. The rest of you—" He turned to Valdez and said, "Where's the doctor?"

"I'll take them," Valdez said.

McNelly looked up at King Fisher, who grinned down at him and said, "Better luck next time, Cap'n."

Chapter Thirty-Seven

"Will you ever be back this way?" Nancy Ward asked. She was sitting up in bed, and although pain was still etched on her face, it was tempered by the fact that the doctor told her that her collarbone had not been splintered and that she should recover fully.

"It's not something I could promise, Nancy, but who knows?" the doctor said.

"Well, thank you for not pressing charges against Douglas, Clint."

"Don't thank me for that," Clint said quickly. "I did it against my better judgment."

"You did it for me, Clint, and I love you for it. Now get out of here. I know you're probably itching to get on the move."

"Nancy, take care of yourself," he said, bending over to kiss her on the forehead.

As he left he hoped that Douglas' experience had

taught him something, and that he wouldn't continue to be a millstone around her neck.

Outside he found Sheriff Valdez waiting for him.

"I guess things haven't changed very much for you," Clint said as Valdez walked him to the livery. "You've still got King Fisher."

"I believe I am better prepared to handle him now, though," Valdez said, "thanks to you. Why do you think he is letting you go without reprisal?"

"I think after everything that's happened he just doesn't believe it's worth the effort anymore. Besides, he's got some housecleaning of his own to do, not to mention Captain McNelly looking over his shoulder waiting for him to make a mistake."

As they approached the livery Valdez touched Clint's arm and jerked his head toward the stable. Clint saw Linda McCall waiting there.

"I'll leave you here," Valdez said.

"Good luck, Sheriff," Clint said, shaking hands with the other man.

"Gracias, and *vaya con dios, amigo."*

As Clint approached the livery Linda took a few steps to meet him.

"Came to say good-bye."

"I'm glad."

"I won't ask you if you'll be back. You probably get enough of that."

She moved close to him and kissed him good-bye soundly.

"I'll be leaving soon too."

"I hope you find what you're looking for, Linda."

"I don't know what I'm looking for," she said honestly. "But, whatever it is I know it's not in Eagle Pass."

"You'll find it."

She watched as he guided his team out of the livery and waved as he directed it north.

One thing Clint was glad about was that he hadn't seen Douglas Ward again in the few days following the showdown with King Fisher's vaqueros. He had only agreed to drop the charges on the condition that he never see Ward again, and Valdez had made that point very clear to the man, so he had dug himself a hole and wouldn't come out until the Gunsmith had left town.

That was where all backshooters belonged anyway—in a hole.

www.ingramcontent.com/pod-product-compliance
Lightning Source LLC
Chambersburg PA
CBHW050735250626
47155CB00005B/1793